Operation Dawn Wolf

An
Agent Carrie Harris
Action Thriller

G J Stevens

British Library Cataloguing-in-Publication Data
A catalogue record for this book is available from the British Library

Cover Copyright © 2021 GJ Stevens
Cover design by Jessica Bell Design
www.gjstevens.com

ISBN: 9781079982169

Other Books by GJ Stevens

Agent Carrie Harris Action Thrillers

LESSON LEARNED
CAPITAL ACTION
THE GEMINI ASSIGNMENT

James Fisher Series

FATE'S AMBITION

Post-apocalyptic Thrillers

IN THE END
BEFORE THE END
AFTER THE END
BEGINNING OF THE END

SURVIVOR – Your Guide to Surviving the Apocalypse

DEDICATION

To the men and woman who tirelessly work to make our world a safer place, putting themselves in harm's way so we can sleep soundly.

ACKNOWLEDGMENTS

To my friends who inspire me every day and sometimes let me work on my passion, despite being on holiday!

Thanks to all those who helped me along the way, be it big or small, I am grateful.

Case File

OPERATION DAWN WOLF

ID65461097-01-ODW

Chronology

Opened:	████ ███ 1998	SECTION A - ~~EYES ONLY~~
Closed:	6th Feb 2001	SECTION A - ~~TOP SECRET~~
Redactions:	20th May 2001	SECTION F - **SECRET**

File Summary

Herein follows the case file for OPERATION DAWN WOLF in the form of audio transcripts from covert recordings, professional journal entries relating to the case, operative reports and miscellaneous files.

20th May 2001

The files contain numerous redactions to protect the identities of current and past operations and operational agents, lowering the security status of the information from TOP SECRET to SECRET.

No details have been changed or edited, however the final report by ██████ ████ ████ cannot be downgraded to SECRET and is therefore omitted.

SECRET – WHEN REDACTED

Candidate Profile   ~~TOP SECRET~~

Candidate:	**HUGHES, Corra**
	██████ ████ (1999) / ████ ███████ (1998)
File-Annex:	C3426109-61
Query Date:	1st August 2000
Current Rank:	Second Lieutenant (1999)
Source File Ref:	D352671-8 & Y-71999210-1

Height:	5' 9" / 175cm
Weight:	119 Pounds / 54kg
Hair:	Blonde, Strawberry. Shoulder length. *[Note: Striking]*
Skin Tone:	IC1 (Pale)
Ethnicity:	BRITISH WHITE
Phys. Condition:	Excellent (Sept 2000)
Men. Condition:	Stable (Sept 2000) (MB Type – INTP)
Past Medical:	(1992) Right Medial Malleolus – Multiple Fractures
	(1999) Appendectomy

Education

Primary:	St Mary's PS, ████████, ████████ (████ – ████)
	St John's PS, ████, ████████ (██████ – ████)
	Merfield PS, ████████, ████████ (████ – ████)
Secondary:	██████ HS, ████████, ████ (████ – ████)
Further:	Welbeck College (1997 – 1998)
Higher:	None
Graduate:	Royal Military Academy Sandhurst (1999)

Service Record:	(████ - 1997) - 5 Pl ████████ ████ █████
	(Army Cadet Corp) – Under Officer
Current Dept:	██ ████
Clearance:	████████ ████████
Commendations:	Winner Chadwick Challenge (1) (1998)
	Sword of Honour (RMAS) (1999)

Notes:	

TRANSCRIPT OF AUDIO RECORDING A1763529-1
[DEVICE C120 COVERT RECORDER]

DL 18th MAY 2001, TS 19th MAY 2001, SECTION D

[DATE:14th SEPT 2000] [10:00GMT]
[LOCATION: ████████████████████ *]*

[Identified as Dr David Devlin (DD), Head of Occupational Psychology, Section A ███████████████ *]*

DD: Good morning.

[Identified as Corra Hughes (CH) (Alias), Candidate Section A (
████████ █████ ███ ████ █, ████ ██
█████████████████ *See File Annex C3426109-*
61, D352671-8, Y-71999210-1)]

CH: Good morning, Mr Devlin.

DD: Doctor, if you don't mind. Take a seat. This conversation is being recorded as an aid memoire for my records.

CH: Okay.

DD: Your name please?

CH: Sorry.

DD: It's fine. Your name?

[Silence]

DD: Is there a problem?

CH: No, it's just…

[Silence]

CH: …sorry. Which do you mean? My real name or the name I've been assigned?

DD: Your most recent name, please.

CH: Yes, sorry. *[Clears throat]* Corra Hughes.

DD: How old are you, Miss Hughes?

CH: Nineteen, and Corra's fine, if you prefer.

DD: Your height?

CH: Five foot and nine inches, or one point seven five metres in new money, as my dad would say.

DD: Weight?

CH: Eight and a half stone, or fifty-four kilos, when I last checked.

DD: Which was when?

CH: On my medical, about two weeks ago.

DD: Any pre-existing medical conditions?

CH: No.

DD: Physical or mental?

CH: No.

DD: Any family history?

CH: My great aunt was a bit loopy, but I don't think it was diagnosed.

DD: Thank you.

CH: I think I've already had a full psych screen?

DD: You have.

[Silence]

DD: Can you tell me what you feel is your best quality?

CH: I'm not sure what you mean?

DD: Okay. Tell me what you like about yourself?

[Silence]

DD: There is no need to be coy. I'm not judging you. I want you to relax. You seem a little nervous.

[Silence]

CH: My physical fitness.

DD: Anything else?

CH: My hair.

DD: Your hair?

CH: Yes. It's different.

DD: Strawberry blonde is the new black.

CH: *[Laughter]* It's individual.

DD: You have a lot to be proud of. Can you not think of anything else?

CH: I don't think so.

DD: What about the rest of your looks? You are very attractive; from an objective perspective, I mean.

CH: Thank you. I don't really think about it.

DD: Okay.

[Silence]

DD: Where should we start? Your file is pretty full.

[Silence]

DD: Oh, yes. I remember reading this. Very interesting.

[Silence]

DD: Okay. What do you remember about your injury?

CH: It hurt.

[Silence]

CH: For a long time.

DD: Yes, I'm sure it did. Maybe you should tell me about how you received the injury.

CH: I got hit by a car.

DD: That's the punchline. Let's go back a bit further. Remember, I'm here to understand you, get to know how you tick, find your motivation and if by doing that I can help you deal with anything that may be lurking in the past, then all the better.

CH: And to decide if I'm right for the job.

DD: This should have been explained to you in your first briefing. We want to see your human side. Perfection is unobtainable. You have flaws, I have flaws. We need to know what they are so we can help deal with them.

        Yes, my reports will be considered as part of the selection process, but look on the bright side; if you don't make it to the end then at least you've had the benefits of a five-hundred-pound-an-hour therapist.

[Silence]

DD: Let's start from the beginning. What is your first memory?

CH: You don't talk like a therapist.

[Silence]

DD: We're having a conversation. I want to keep this light and put you at ease.

CH: Perhaps you could hang some pictures, string a few lights and maybe get a potted plant or two if you want to put me at ease. Having a conversation with someone in what resembles a cell from *The Green Mile* is not really making me feel comfortable.

DD: I can't do anything about the surroundings, I'm afraid. Your first memory?

[Silence]

CH: It's just a snapshot; a picture in my head. It's a hospital, I think, and I'm about four or five. It's difficult to tell.

        My father was a Crab, so we moved around a lot. I have several houses and places in there, but it's not always clear where they were.

DD: Is this when you had your injury?

CH: No. I was much older. Thirteen.

DD: Why were you in the hospital?

CH: I don't remember.

DD: Did you ever ask your parents?

CH: No. It's just an image in my head. It might not even have been me; it might have been the birth of my sister. It would kind of fit.

DD: What's a Crab?

CH: A crustacean, walks sideways. *[Laughter]* Sorry. It's an unkind name given to people in the RAF. I thought you…

[Silence]

CH: …never mind.

DD: We are not a military organisation.

CH: Okay.

7

DD: Why do you choose to use an unkind word to describe your father?

[Silence]

DD: Okay. What about school?

CH: Schools, plural. I remember clearly when we moved to the last place my parents eventually settled in. It was my dad's last posting as he'd decided to go for PVR after twenty-two years and they were looking to buy the last house they would ever need.

My parents had been clever. Most forces families lived in married quarters, which is great at the time, but when you leave you have nothing. For as long as I can remember I've always lived off base. My parents were nearly mortgage free when he decided to leave and we were spared the usual shock of having to start from scratch. It's kind of like I knew this would be a place I could make roots, so my head let the memories stick.

[Silence]

DD: PVR?

CH: Sorry. Early retirement.

DD: And the accident? From the start please.

CH: My last year at primary school was a good time for the most part. I made friends, which I'd always found easy and it's where I first gained an interest in gymnastics. They ran a class after school, which soon turned into weekends with a local club. Secondary school started much the same way. The PE department were happy to help me keep up with what had become a passion.

A teacher, Miss Peters, recognised I had a talent and soon pushed for me to train with the county team. I came second in the county in the year's headline competition and new friends were coming along all of the time.

PE teachers were taking time out to help me after school and ferry me around my training when my parents weren't able. Dad was starting a new job and putting the hours in. Mum worked too, back then.

It was at one of the early season competitions that things kind of went a bit sour.

DD: How old were you?

CH: I must have only been twelve. It was towards the end of the very long day. I was off form and not doing very well; about mid table with nearly too much to make up to stay in contention. I only had one more apparatus to go, the balance beam. I went to the bathroom, which was near a set of double doors. A fire escape or something like that.

DD: Where was the event held?

CH: At a school on the edge of the county. I forget its name and I'd never been there before. The fire doors were open and there was a small van parked with the engine running and its double doors open at the back. I remember coughing at the fumes from the exhaust and thinking it was a little odd, but I was distracted, concentrating on running through my routine in my head.

Anyway, I had to pee with only minutes until my next round. When I'd finished in the cubicle, I saw a man standing staring straight at me and before I could think, he snatched his arms around my waist.

[Silence]

DD: Are you okay to carry on?

CH: Yes fine. I was pretty small back then, and slim; an

9

easy weight for a big guy to carry. He covered my mouth and I couldn't scream. I remember trying to breath, but his hand was over my nose and mouth. What little breath I did catch stank of coffee and stale cigarettes.

I remember vividly the stars dancing out in front of my eyes as we came out of the corridor and towards the van with my arms pinned tight at my sides. I saw blankets laid out on the floor as he threw himself in, screaming at the driver to go and still holding me tight.

The last of my breath was knocked out of me. I barely noticed as we almost rolled straight back out as the van shot away, the back doors still open.

DD: What was going through your mind when this was all happening?

[Silence]

CH: I remember not feeling scared. I was more annoyed, so utterly pissed off I was going to miss the chance for my final piece and to try and make up the deficit.

DD: Take a deep breath.

[Silence]

CH: Sorry. The memories are very clear. I was on the edge of blacking out and I caught sight of Miss Peters in the corridor. She was shrinking into the distance. I'll always remember the abject horror on her face.

Somehow her look spurred me on, making me realise what was happening and I did the only thing I could think to do. I went limp. I had to concentrate hard to stop myself going out. He must have realised I couldn't breathe and thought I was unconscious because he loosened his hand. I pulled in a massive breath that stank of cigarettes, but I didn't wait. The doors were still open and I bit his hand as hard as I could.

He instantly pulled away with both hands.

[Silence]

CH: The rest is mostly a blur; all I remember is my elbow connecting with his nose and a rather satisfying noise of his flesh and my relief as he let go. The momentum carried me out of the van and I rolled on the tarmac, landing in a crouch on my feet, panting as the van roared away into the distance. Miss Peter's ran to me, screaming and almost hysterical, collecting me up.

[Silence]

DD: You sound like you've told that story before.

CH: Just a few times. To the police and councillors over the years.

DD: Then what happened?

CH: She took me back into the school.

DD: How did Miss Peters react?

CH: I think she went into shock, in particular over how calm I was as I explained what had happened. A raft of police cars and an ambulance soon came and everyone fussed around me. They found no injuries, apart from a sore mouth where I had bitten him so hard. Still, they wanted me to go home.

DD: And you didn't?

CH: No, and it was at that point I got upset. Great respect to Miss Peters; she knew how much it meant to me and convinced the organisers to let me finish competing. Everyone had stayed because they'd delayed the competition for over an hour while it was all going on.

11

DD: Did you compete?

CH: I did.

DD: And?

CH: And what?

DD: Where did you finish?

CH: First. I got my highest ever score, personal best. Broke the county record, nearly the national for my age.

DD: Wow.

CH: Thank you. I guess.

DD: Did they catch them?

CH: No. The police visited a few days later and told me and my parents it was just opportunists. Wrong place, wrong time, that sort of thing.

DD: But you didn't believe them?

CH: I did. Until the next time.

DD: Please tell. Take your time.

[Silence]

CH: Breaking the county record got me assigned a coach.

[Silence]

CH: Coach ███.

DD: What makes you smile when you remember him?

CH: He was a really cool guy. He was one of the first adults I could call by his first name and not Mr ███.
        He enrolled me on a self-defence course, a mix of Aikido and Jujitsu; didn't even ask me if it was something I wanted to do. He thought I was lacking

confidence after what had happened. Turned out he was right. I loved the course and I quickly began to feel so much better in myself.

If it wasn't for the commitment required for the gymnastics, I think I would have taken it further there and then.

Gymnastics went from strength to strength, my scoring consistently rising; so much so I was invited to train with the junior GB team. There were whispers of the Olympics in Atlanta, but I never did beat my PB.

I came close the next year, but couldn't quite get there in time.

DD: What changed since the incident?

CH: They called it an attempted kidnap, if anyone dared to say something about it in my earshot and especially in my mother's. To me, it was a distant memory. I'd nearly blocked it out, although no one else around me seemed to have.

Whenever we were in competition, I would be chaperoned everywhere I went, especially to the toilets; the venues always seemed to have their toilets down some dark and dingy corridors.

DD: Did that provoke a reaction?

CH: Not in me.

[Silence]

CH: Anyway, I was in competition, junior selections of the national squad at the European Championships, my first selection event at that level. I was so excited. I was in the low stands of probably the biggest gym I'd ever seen, some secondary school in Berkshire, when I thought I saw the guy who'd tried to grab me.

DD: What did you do?

13

CH: I looked away.

[Silence]

CH: It hadn't sunk in what I'd seen, but as my brain caught up and I looked back, it must have been less than a second later. He was gone. I'd seen him, I was sure, but I convinced myself it was the competition nerves playing tricks. My third session was about to start on the Pommel Horse.

          I needed to pee; kind of a habit. I used to try and go every second piece of apparatus. You drink so much to keep hydrated and then it turned into a ritual. You know what sports people are like for their superstitions. If I didn't go and went on to have a bad day, it would be my own fault.

[Silence]

CH: Too much information. Sorry.

DD: It's okay.

CH: I checked around, but my teammates were either warming up or on the apparatus, Mum was off getting coffee and ███████ was over the other side of the gym talking to one of the other girls he was coaching. There was no way I could perform with a full bladder so I headed off to the bathroom.

          He was already in there as I went through the doorway.

DD: It was same guy?

CH: Yes. We looked at each other. I was frozen to the spot. He didn't move, just looked at me and seemed to be smiling.

DD: Smiling? What sort of smile?

CH: It wasn't as sinister as it sounds. It seemed like a genuine smile. Which was odd, but that's the only way

14

I can describe it. He looked pleased to see me and I don't mean in some psycho way.

DD: Then what happened?

CH: The door opened behind me. The moment broke and I was struck with a feeling of elation; it would be my mum looking for me. I imagined her scowling, coffee in hand, ready to rip a strip off me for going off on my own.

DD: It wasn't your mum.

CH: No.

DD: Who was it?

CH: I don't know. All I saw was the edge of a blanket. Everything went dark as it covered my head. Thick, heavy arms gripped around my chest, pinning my elbows to my sides. I was turned, really manhandled, my head pushed into what felt like the loose fat of a chest, a hand pushing behind me.

DD: Was it different to last time?

CH: Yes. It felt so much rougher. I remember them shouting at each other but the detail was muffled by the blanket. I was lifted off my feet, bouncing up and down as he ran with me, his hands clamping me closer.

        Everything was happening at the same time. I swung my legs wildly, my feet hitting at shins, but the stupid beam shoes coach made me wear were so flimsy. I may as well have been barefoot.

        I forced myself to calm, trying to remember what I'd been taught. I nearly couldn't control myself, the grip around me tightening as my body relaxed and I felt the urgent need to pee.

DD: Did the self-defence help?

CH: We'd learnt to try and bend your back, so I did, all whilst trying to stamp on his feet, but my legs were in the air. I didn't know how high up I was. I couldn't think clearly and leant back, relaxing further. I swung my head forward, trying to gain as much height as I could. My forehead connected to something soft and the grip fell from around me.

I can still hear his dull moan.

As my feet hit the floor I ran forward, shoulder barging the bulk to the side. I could feel the weight staggering back and I stamped my feet as I heard the one who had me fall to the floor. I kicked out and connected with something soft. He cried out in pain. I ran, my hand flailing to get the blanket off, which I did just in time to see I was about to run straight into a wall.

I'd run the wrong way. As I turned, I saw the wide doors of a fire escape, the bulk of a third person striding towards me.

I could see in his expression he wasn't going to save me. I glanced over my shoulder to see the first guy was leaving blood in his footsteps as he chased after me; his friend, and where the blood was coming from, was climbing to his feet. I screamed, the echo ringing through the corridor, but they didn't flinch. They were going to get me, I was sure.

[Silence]

DD: Do you want a break?

CH: No, it's fine. Thank you.

I ran for the lone guy in front of the doorway. He was fat and slow and I easily passed him and pushed open the fire doors already slightly ajar.

I ran and ran, looking behind me and only saw the car when it was nearly too late. I bounded up, my foot caught on the bonnet and it flipped me over. As I landed on both feet, my right gave no resistance to the ground and I felt it shorten as pain seared up my leg.

[Silence]

CH: Gymnastics had saved my life and all I could think wasn't that I was a sitting target, but that my dreams had all come to an end.

[Silence]

DD: Take your time. The assailants made off?

CH: Yes. The car was nothing to do with them and although the driver couldn't understand at the time, hitting it stopped me going through whatever they had in store.

DD: Was it as bad as it seemed? The ankle I mean.

CH: Yes. Worse even. I had to undergo three different surgeries to get it straightened. It took six months of rest and physio to get back to walking. Another six to lose the pirate limp.

DD: How were you after?

CH: Gutted. Gymnastics was over and all I did was mope around the house. I was piling on the pounds as my mum wouldn't let me out of her sight. She had a burglar alarm installed in the house and a panic button linked to the local police station in every room.

DD: That's a hell of a hole. How did you climb out?

CH: ▆▆▆▆ and Miss Peters. I was back in school after a month and he visited every other week. He saw my leg getting better and the fat building, each week losing more and more of what he said was my sparkle. I wasn't willing to join in with any of the activities people kept asking me to take up.

It was him who told me about the army cadets.

DD: What was your first reaction to his suggestion?

CH: I laughed it off, but he persisted, bringing me leaflets and stories of all the fun crazy things I'd get to do. He'd already had a word with a friend who was a volunteer and he told me that when I was walking again, I could go along to see what it was like.

But let's just say I was less than keen.

DD: In what way?

CH: I didn't want to do anything, but on the other hand I felt trapped and this felt like it was just another way to keep me caged. Every day my mum would drop me at the school gates, watching until I disappeared around the school buildings and out of view. She rang my form tutor every lunch time to check I was okay.

Twice she turned up at the office demanding to see me in the middle of my lessons after break as my tutor was off sick and the school office had forgotten to call her back. I could have died of embarrassment. I was ready to sink into the start of my teenage years as a recluse.

DD: What changed?

CH: I saw him again. Well I thought I saw him again.

DD: Go on.

CH: My mum was late. I think I must have been the last in school. I was waiting inside the school gates; if I was seen anywhere else it would have sent my mum into an early grave.

I saw him drive by in a van. He looked at me. Our eyes met.

DD: Was it definitely him?

18

CH: I don't know. I was sure at the time, but the white van, it was dark inside; it's difficult to be sure when I look back.

        Anyway, Mum turned up, apologetic, telling me what a good girl I was for staying safe. I blurted it out. I told her that I was going to see what the army cadets were like.

DD: How did she react?

CH: She put up a protest of course, but coach had already spoken to her and she didn't try too hard. The cadets actually met at the barracks down the road.

DD: Where else would you have an armed guard on high alert at the time for Irish terrorists?

CH: Exactly. She'd seen me dropping too, losing my spirit.

[Silence]

DD: And I see you didn't like it. *[Laughter]*

CH: *[Laughter]* Yeah. You might say that I found my second calling.

DD: You could say that. Cadet Corporal within six months, CCSM within two years, Under Officer before you left.

CH: Yeah. It was an amazing few years. All that time I'd previously put into gymnastics now went into the cadets. The leaders weren't really ready for my enthusiasm, but most of them were ex-army and knew the regiments on base, so between them they were able to accommodate my appetite.

        They even got some of the serving soldiers involved, each one volunteering to help us out on the range and drill, that sort of thing. We did so much as a troop; climbing mountains, going on camp, sports competitions, the shooting range, that kind of thing.

DD: It says here that the detachment was the most active out of any in the country, including having the highest number of recruits during the years you were there.

CH: Yes. Loads of people from school followed me in; the school even let me do a recruiting day during lunch hours. When we had the Air Corp land two Lynx on the school fields, we signed up another twenty cadets that day alone. They even had to expand it beyond the one night a week because the groups were just too big.

DD: And did you see him again?

[Silence]

CH: Probably once or twice a year.

DD: Did you ever tell anyone?

CH: Twice.

DD: Who?

CH: My parents.

DD: And?

CH: The police came, but by the time they arrived he was long gone. I felt such a fraud and a drain on resources. Each time they came, my parents would lose their shit. My mum would get so anxious and her control over me would tighten.

DD: You stopped telling people?

CH: Despite all of the sightings, my confidence was through the roof.

DD: Why?

CH: I'd been learning self-defence with the Corp, building on what I knew already. I could keep myself safe, stay out of dangerous situations.

  We'd been given introductions to reconnaissance from specialists from the brigade. It turned out I was already very observant and it only improved as I progressed.

  I saw the signs. It got to a stage where I was willing him to try it again.

DD: Sorry. Explain please. You wanted him to try and abduct you again?

[Silence]

CH: I carried a knife. A concealed three-inch blade just for him and I knew how to use it. But I wasn't stupid. I kept myself out of dangerous situations.

DD: So much to say, but where to start. You realise the attention you received in the cadets, the training, the extra hours and all these people helping you out isn't normal?

CH: I do now.

[Silence]

DD: Do you still see him?

[Silence]

CH: No.

DD: You're not convincing me.

[Silence]

CH: Okay. I do see him, but I guess you would say he wasn't really there.

DD: Are you after my job?

CH: *[Laughter]* I think I see him because I want to. I want it to be real so my mind is helping me.

DD: What makes you say that?

CH: He's ageing. Each time I see him he's that little bit
        older. Deeper lines around his eyes. His hair is
        greying. It's been seven years since I first saw him and
        in my head he's not ageing well.

DD: Have you given any thought as to who it might be?

CH: An understatement.

DD: And?

CH: First thought was some paedo with a fascination for
        gymnasts, but there were two of them, three on the
        last attempt, so it would have to be a gang. Then it
        was white slavers, but I thought it all started a bit
        young and was probably an urban myth. But you're
        raising your eyebrows, so I guess not.
                I thought about common garden kidnappers
        looking for a ransom, but my family have no money.
        Then Irish republican or Islamic terrorists maybe
        because of my dad serving in the forces.
                We were always being told to look under our
        cars and to be vigilant for suspect packages. I kind of
        got stuck there for a long while.

DD: Did you discuss your thoughts with anyone?

CH: I told the police but they dismissed my ideas as
        fantasies. When the DNA didn't come back with
        anyone, they said the truth would be much more
        mundane. Probably just a nut job, I'm paraphrasing,
        with a fascination and he would likely grow bored and
        move on.

DD: How did that make you feel?

CH: It wasn't an answer. They didn't know. Too many
        times they said 'thought' and 'probably' and when
        they said he would move on it wouldn't be a close. If

he moved on to someone else, I wouldn't be able to forgive myself.

DD: Why?

CH: Because we didn't catch him.

DD: We? He's not your responsibility.

CH: You know what I mean.

[Silence]

DD: What are you thinking?

CH: Another scenario just came into my head. *[Laughter]*

DD: And?

CH: He was with your lot.

DD: What makes you say that?

CH: I saw him on the first evasion exercise.

DD: Evasion One, yes. You seemed to do rather well.

[Silence]

DD: Don't be coy now. I'm very impressed. Tell me about it.

CH: *[Laughter]* Where should I start?

DD: At the beginning, of course. Start from when you found out you were going on exercise so quickly after arriving here.

CH: By the noises in the room people were pretty shocked. Clearly none of us were expecting things to kick off so quickly.

        Even those of us who had some inkling were shocked.

        We'd been here for less than an hour, the

briefing had just finished and we were out on our heels, piled into a van with a load of strangers. With barely enough time for a few words between us in the minibus, we were shoved out on our own.

DD: But still you're smiling.

CH: Yep. Loved it.

DD: And they weren't all strangers.

CH: No. I had three fellow graduate officers with me.

DD: Ah yes, you entered Sandhurst without a degree. How did that come about?

[Silence]

DD: Okay. I'm sure it's in your file somewhere. It must have been comforting to have three friends with you.

CH: One of them I could call a friend.

DD: Ah, yes, Fifty-Four.

CH: Stacey, yes. She was in the year above me at Welbeck and we ended up in the same company together at Sandhurst.

DD: Welbeck?

CH: It's the Defence Sixth Form College.

DD: Oh, okay. Like your everyday college but with guns?

CH: Kind of yes, plus additional training in technical areas for various branches of the forces.

DD: What was Welbeck like?

CH: Have you heard of Harry Potter?

DD: My children have read it. How many books is it now?

CH: Book four came out a few months ago. I haven't had

a chance to pick it up yet.

[Silence]

DD: I'm missing the original point.

CH: Most of the story is based around a school. Hogwarts. It's where the wizards go off to learn magic and unearth conspiracies. Anyway, it's a cross between a castle and a stately home. That's what Welbeck was like, but without the magic or a proper maintenance budget. Lots of dark rooms and vaults which someone thought would be great to turn into a college.

DD: Right.

[Silence]

DD: Back to Stacey. Are you close?

[Silence]

CH: She's about as close a friend as I've ever had.

DD: And the other two?

CH: Not so much. I keep a close circle.

DD: How many are in that circle?

CH: Well it's more like a line, or a dot.

DD: She's your only friend.

[Silence]

DD: After the briefing they put you out into the cold?

CH: Yes. They gave each of us a rucksack with a few supplies and the clothes we arrived in. I was prepared, wearing walking boots, combat trousers, a fleece and jacket. The others not so much. Suits and ties.

DD: Did you know what was going to happen?

CH: No. I just came prepared. I knew it wasn't a skirt and blouse type of interview.

DD: And if you'd been wrong?

CH: Then it wasn't the job for me.

DD: What happened after you were dropped off?

CH: There were thirteen of us in the minibus, no sign of the other three vehicles. I headed straight towards a village we could see on the horizon. All we knew was there was only half an hour before they would begin tracking us, so Stacey and I were light on our feet.

DD: Was she prepared for the exercise?

CH: Unfortunately not. We hadn't spoken since Sandhurst; none of us had. I didn't know she was going to be there, so I couldn't tell her what I thought.

DD: Carry on.

CH: As we headed to the village, it looked like the others, except for a Desmond, had the same idea.

DD: You'll need to excuse my ignorance. Desmond?

CH: Tu Tu. Twenty-two squadron.

DD: With the greatest of respect, aren't you a little inexperienced to be using that slang and how do you know he was SAS?

CH: I've been associated with the military now for almost six years, plus I watched a lot of TV. He had that air, a look in his eye and he wouldn't stop taking the piss out of everyone, until he was out of the van of course. He left his pack behind and made his own way, soon disappeared down into a valley.

26

DD: Have you had experience with special forces operatives before?

CH: Yes. They were involved on some of the training exercises. The Paras are big and loud, showing off to everyone who looked, but the special forces guys were small and quiet, and ignored everyone else. They were easy to spot in that big lecture theatre. There were a lot of them too, spooks as well.

DD: How do you know?

CH: It stands to reason. I probably have a better idea of what this is all about than most. I wouldn't come along until they told me at least the barest details. The recruiting pool makes perfect sense. Lots of people you'd forget in a flash. Everyone was fit. With my hair I think I stood out the most.

DD: It is rather striking.

CH: They were all observant, switched on, taking it all in while trying to look like they weren't, but the SF guys looked ready for it, ready to take it on. The spooks looked like they wanted to hide under a rock. There were a few civvies too, and regulars. I spotted a pilot, which was a surprise, and a few engineers.

[Silence]

DD: How do you know?

CH: Difficult to describe. It's a lateral conclusion. I'm observant, I've been told once or twice.

DD: How much do you know about this process?

CH: Not much. But I was invited here so I know a little. Like I said, I wasn't going to come unless they gave me some idea of what it was going to be.

DD: Everyone is here by invitation.

27

CH: Um, can we take a break?

DD: Yes, sure. Then we can get back to Evasion One.

Journal of Dr Devlin, Head of Occupational Psychology

Section A ████████████████

14th September 2000 - Session 1.1

Initial Opinions

Ms H is likeable. A bit disconnected is probably the only way I can describe her, but certainly likeable. I can see why she inspires people, such as ████, her teacher and the cadet leadership team to want to help and facilitate her growth. I find myself very much in her corner, although acutely aware that I must stay objective.

She seems to have dealt with her horrific childhood experiences well, in the most part. Perhaps this is the reason for the disconnection. She also appears to have an understanding that her attempted abductor has become a metaphor and her subconscious is using him almost as a support blanket, which she utilises to drive her on.

The relationship with Stacey is interesting. For someone who is so likeable, she only has one real friend. Explore this further. Does this affect her ability to work in a team? We don't just need people who are lone wolves.

It's interesting that Ms H likes the Harry Potter novels, which are essentially children's books. I'm not sure how significant this is but I will explore this further.

I get the impression that Ms H is holding back. It is still our first session so I expect that to change. During this session I have noted several times that whenever she mentions her coach, she gives a reaction, an almost imperceivable tell. I will explore this further.

TRANSCRIPT OF AUDIO RECORDING A1763529-1
[DEVICE C120 COVERT RECORDER]

[DATE:14th SEPT 2000] [11:30GMT]
[LOCATION: ██████████████████████ *]*

DD: Ah. There you are? Did you get lost?

CH: No. Sorry. I had something to take care of and I lost track of time.

DD: Okay. No problem. Let's get back into this.

[Silence]

DD: Where were we? Yes. Did one of your lot steal a car?

CH: Stacey. In the first village she pulled open one of the house doors that wasn't locked and grabbed the keys.

DD: Then gave them away.

CH: She gave them to me and I gave them away.

DD: Why?

CH: I put the phone from my pack in the boot. I wanted it away from me as quick as possible.

DD: Why? Everyone was carrying phones.

CH: Just in case I was singled out.

DD: You think they can track you with the phone.

CH: Do you understand how mobile phones work?

DD: No.

CH: I do and from what I know they can be used to get a good idea of where you are between the cell towers, and that's just the kit that's commercially available.

DD: Okay. I'll take your lead on that. Do you think you have been singled out?

CH: It was a precaution.

DD: And now?

CH: Now I know I am. I've put my head above the parapet, so to speak.

DD: Yes. We'll get to that. And you did this at the expense of the other team?

CH: It was an individual exercise. That was made clear as they first broke the news. If it had been a team challenge, I would have acted differently.

DD: They were captured within an hour.

[Silence]

DD: Don't you feel bad?

CH: Are you telling me I should?

DD: No. Not at all. Do you feel any emotion at getting your fellow candidates caught?

CH: Are you telling me it was possible to track the phone? Was it the reason they were caught?

[Silence]

DD: I have no idea. But let's say your actions led directly, or indirectly to their capture. Does that make you feel some responsibility or regret?

CH: Why would I? They should have shown better craft than to leave themselves exposed. If it was me, I would have noticed the phone and I wouldn't have let someone else risk my success on the exercise.

DD: Is that the only reason?

CH: What other reason could there be?

[Silence]

DD: How did you get out of Talybont-on-Usk?

CH: Back of a CO-OP lorry. It was left unattended while
        it was loading up. Three of us, Stacey and a spook.
        We hid deep in the back amongst the trolleys.

DD: So not everyone went in the car?

CH: No.

DD: And the guy with you didn't identify himself?

CH: No.

DD: But you let him come along for the ride?

CH: No reason not to. There was room for three, a fourth
        couldn't fit and he had to go.

DD: Then?

CH: We arrived in Brecon.

DD: It must have been cold in the back of the truck.

CH: Yes. We were glad to get out. We exchanged our
        dollars and got a taxi to Hereford. The spook didn't
        want to go along, which was fine by me.

DD: Did you see any risk in what you did?

CH: We knew changing the dollars could be a risk, but it
        was better than trying to pass off the fake fifties we
        were given in the pack.

DD: Just to be clear, I am not part of the instruction team.
        My role is almost independent.

[Silence]

DD: You can raise your eyebrows all you want, but it's
        true. Why was changing the dollars such a risk?

CH: Why give them to us if there wasn't some sort of

notification when and where they were converted? An electronic record of the serial numbers maybe. How quick it would be we weren't sure, so we changed them as close to where you, sorry, *they* knew we would be.

DD: Perhaps they were just there to confuse you, or make you paranoid about the point of giving you the dollars. Was it working?

CH: Do you mean was I being paranoid?

[Silence]

CH: I was being careful. Considering all of the scenarios.

DD: And the taxi?

CH: We booked it to head to Llandrindod Wells, but changed it to Hereford once it arrived. I told some sob story about an abusive boyfriend so he wouldn't tell the controller.

[Silence]

CH: So why are you here?

DD: As I said before, I'm here to understand you and I do that through conversation. I have nothing to do with what the instructors are doing and this has no bearing on what they are looking for in you. They have no influence on me and I none on them. In fact, I barely have any contact with any of the rest of the team.

CH: Ah. I see. You want me to disassociate you with the people who were trying to hunt me down, the people that wake me every day at four AM and push me past my limits so it doesn't affect the rapport you're trying to build so I'll open up.

[Silence]

33

CH: Okay. I'll play along if you like.

        We split up in Hereford. I bought a train ticket to Birmingham, waited for the train, boarded on the first carriage, but got off last minute at the other end of the train.

DD: Now that I did hear about. CAPOP fell for that one. They missed your exit because it was covered by a separate CCTV camera which they didn't have eyes on. He'd already swept up over half of the candidates and assigned three of the mobile teams to make sure they could pick you up.

        It must have been over half an hour before he figured out what you'd done and found you on the footage, but by that time you'd pushed all of his team out of place. They tried tracking you out of the station, but after you walked out, they lost you.

[Silence]

DD: Had you disguised yourself?

CH: No. Not at this stage. We hadn't had the time. It was a risk and I knew there was a good chance the train stations would be under surveillance or they'd roll-back the CCTV. Hence the tactic.

DD: Then why go there at all?

CH: Maybe to mess with them a little.

[Silence]

DD: Well you did mess with them quite a lot. Was it worth the risk? Did you gain any operational benefit or was it just for kicks?

CH: We tied up a load of their teams chasing after shadows.

[Silence]

DD: How did you get away from the station without being spotted?

CH: While I was in the station, Stacey picked up a ride. Some guy who thought he was going to get more than her thanks when we got to Ross-On-Wye.

DD: The opposite direction. Very good.

CH: Yes. In Ross, we got Stacey a change of clothes. Swapped out her suit for something more sensible at a charity shop, then hitched a ride in the cab of a lorry with a very nice lady. Unfortunately, her tacho made her stop after a couple of hours at a service station just outside of Birmingham, so rather than be exposed, we moved on.
        I caught sight of one of the civvies from the briefing trawling the line of parked trucks for a ride. We knew a team would be on their way.

DD: How did you know? He was detained at 12:57.

CH: I thought you didn't have access to that kind of operation information.

DD: He was my last interviewee before you. How did you know he would be picked up?

[Silence]

CH: Is he still on the course?

DD: Not my decision.

[Silence]

CH: It's a major transport hub on a motorway out of the area. It stands to reason they'd be accessing the CCTV. The guy wasn't being very discrete.

[Silence]

DD: What are you thinking?

CH: 12:57. That was closer than I thought. We must have only just left on another truck.

DD: Tell me about who was driving the second lorry.

CH: Some guy who pretty much had a hard on for Stacey the entire two hours. Much to his protests, we had him drop us on the outskirts of Manchester, a short walk from some new trendy business development.

DD: Then what?

CH: We found a cafe and sat outside.

[Silence]

DD: Then?

CH: We had coffee.

[Silence]

DD: You saw him, didn't you?

CH: Yes.

[Silence]

DD: Did Stacey see him?

[Silence]

CH: You think he's inside my head, don't you?

DD: It just seems a little unlikely that he'd tracked you to Manchester. Especially when there is already a professional team chasing you down who haven't got the first idea where you are.

CH: Sure. I get that.

DD: So what happened?

[Silence]

CH: The cafe was only small, but had a wide seating area. There were a few business types sitting around gassing and eating. The place was a new build, loads of two or three storey blocks all huddled around a landscaped hill with a large pond in the middle. Stacey was in the toilets and I was pretty relaxed now we'd put some distance between us and Wales, but my guard was still up and I had an eye on everything.

DD: It's interesting that you saw him when Stacey wasn't there.

[Silence]

CH: I could see everyone and everything approaching and leaving. The place was pretty stagnant. No reason for any other people to be there other than those visiting or working in the buildings. It was busy enough that we weren't alone, but quiet enough that I could keep a good track.

        One minute he wasn't there, the next minute he was on the other side of the pond staring right at me. I kept my eyes fixed on him, ready to leave when Stacey was done. I didn't have to wait long. I turned to speak to her and was getting up to leave, but when I looked back, he was gone.

[Silence]

CH: Is he with you?

DD: As I say, I don't have access to that kind of operational information I'm afraid.

CH: Okay. Do you think he could be with you?

DD: There are multiple reasons for his appearance, but I think him being part of the capture team is extremely unlikely. Do you think the recruitment unit would put you through all of that?

CH: Granted it is a little extreme, but you've read my file. You know how I was selected for this process.

DD: You're only one of many candidates assigned to me. Let's take a break for lunch, then you can tell me all about it in your own words. Be back at 1330 hours please.

Journal of Dr Devlin, Head of Occupational Psychology

Section A ███████████████

14ᵗʰ September 2000 - Session 1.2

Initial Opinions Cont'd

Ms H was late for our session resuming. This would be unusual in any of the candidates as they are normally so prompt and conscientious, not knowing if any little slip-up could get them kicked off the course. When questioned, she did not freely give the details of the reason for being late.

She exhibits early signs of paranoia; again, not unusual and part of the design of some parts of the course. However, this is very early to be having these feelings.

She is able to disconnect emotionally from other people very easily and has borderline socio / psychopath traits. Each of these is not unusual in the role we are recruiting for; however, it needs to be explored much further and a detailed risk assessment carried out. There was no note of this on her screening.

She displays a level of arrogance just a little higher than the typical candidates. This could be because of everything she has been through and what she has gone on to achieve after. It is likely that should she proceed through the process we would see that arrogance drawing back somewhat.

Ms H is very vocal in her opinions and although happy to share her direct thoughts, despite the weight she knows I have on her success in the process, she is candid whilst still remaining respectful. This said, she still seems to be holding something back.

Despite all my notes so far, it is clear she takes great pleasure in this process and especially in besting the instructor team, such as the unnecessary risk at the train station. I would be mindful of her not putting herself at risk, or her objective, to seek enjoyment.

I can't get a sense of the reality of the stalker. As I talk to her, I feel more and more that he is in her head. Ms H understands this, but I have no doubt she believes she sees him. This is clear because she is in the most part happy to talk about him and the experiences of seeing him, also in the way she questions whether his appearances are part of the exercise. I am yet to make judgement on how this affects her suitability, but it needs to be explored further.

TRANSCRIPT OF AUDIO RECORDING A1763529-1
[DEVICE C120 COVERT RECORDER]

[DATE:14th SEPT 2000] [13:30GMT]
[LOCATION: ████████████████████ *]*

DD: Thank you for coming back promptly. You were about to tell me how you were recruited for this process.

CH: What do you want to know?

DD: Just tell me what happened from the start.

[Silence]

CH: It's a long story. Are you sure you have time?

DD: Let me worry about that.

[Silence]

CH: It was the end of the second term of my final year. I was working on a Design & Technology A-Level project, doing some calculations in the prep room, which was kind of a classroom, but the teachers would use it as a staff area for the department.

DD: What were you making?

CH: It's not relevant.

DD: I would still like to know.

[Silence]

CH: A perimeter security system for the battlefield.

DD: That sounds inter…

CH: I was rushing through the calcs for the practical next period and I was behind for some reason. I can't recall why. Anyway, as I printed off my results, I found a page already in the printer. I glanced to see if

41

it had been printed by one of the other students who'd been in the room with me about half an hour before, but it had no obvious owner and didn't relate to the projects I knew they were working on.

About to place it back, some of the content caught my eye and I was a little surprised to see it was some sort of schematic for a missile. This in itself was nothing unusual, being a military technical college a lot of what we did had a heavy military bias, but we were forbidden from making any overtly offensive technologies, such as weapons, at that time. I'd also never seen or heard of this weapon before.

DD: And you're generally acquainted with missile technology?

CH: Hands up. I'm a bit of a geek. Partly from my family's military background and my own interests. I could play weapons top trumps without any cards.

DD: No harm in that. So you were confident the weapon wasn't on the market?

CH: Yes. The dates of the drawing were only six months ago and the drawing block had Matra BAe Dynamics all over it.

DD: Who are they?

CH: A joint British and French missile manufacturer, recently bought out by BAe Systems, British defence contractor. You must have heard of them?

DD: Yes.

[Silence]

DD: Okay. I get the intrigue. What did you do with it?

CH: I put it back on the printer and as I did, the door opened. One of the staff, a French visiting lecturer called Monsieur Dubois came through, scowling as he saw me. It wasn't unusual for me to be there, but I understood his concern as soon as he snatched the page from the printer's tray. He asked me if I'd touched the paper. I shook my head as I pushed my folders in to my bag and left quickly for my lesson.

[Silence]

DD: How did you feel after that?

CH: Intrigued, I guess, but I'd pretty much put it to the back of my mind by the end of the next lesson. We were mad busy getting plans put together for our coursework assignments. It wasn't until I remembered I'd left something in the prep room and my stomach kind of sank as I realised I'd have to get it.

DD: You could have just left whatever it was there?

CH: No. It was my coursework for the next lesson. I wasn't willing to be that kind of person just because I was nervous of Dubois's reaction.

DD: So you went back?

CH: Yes. I was apprehensive so I approached the closed door slowly at first, but didn't need to get too close to hear a raised voice on the other side of the door. I held back, hovering outside, making sure no one was coming down the corridor.

DD: What were they saying?

CH: The words were in a foreign language. I could tell they weren't in French or German and they were one sided; whoever was on the other end of the line was given no time to talk before the phone slammed against the handset.

        As I heard the conversation end, I ducked into an empty classroom next door. My instinct was

right; it was only a few seconds before the prep room
door flew open and I head footsteps stomping away
down the corridor. As I came out of the classroom, I
saw Dubois's back disappear through the double
doors at the end of the corridor. I nipped into the
office and grabbed the folder from where I'd left it.

DD: So after you left, what triggered your interest again?

CH: I hadn't left yet. It seems really stupid now, but at the
time I couldn't take my eyes off the phone and before
I knew it, I was flicking through the controls,
scribbling down the last incoming call. As I wrote the
last digit for the London number, I flew out of the
prep room and bumped into one of my room mates.
I don't know what she must have thought I'd been
doing, but she said I was bright red, like I'd just run
around the block.

DD: What did you tell her?

CH: I didn't tell her anything. She started talking about
some party she was planning in the Christmas break
and I let myself get absorbed, deliberately losing my
train of thought. It wasn't until I was back at the
boarding house at the end of the day and I saw the
number scribbled in the margin of my lecture notes
that the adrenaline started to surge again.

        I memorised the number and headed out to
the phone in the refectory. It was a busy place right
up till it closed at nine and there were no cameras, so
no way to link the call anywhere near me.

        I had to wait five minutes for the phone to
come free, which was even better as it linked someone
else to the phone around the same time, plus it gave
me chance to calm down.

DD: Who did you call?

CH: First I called directory enquiries to do a reverse

44

lookup, but that came back unlisted. I thought about swapping phones just in case my enquiry had triggered some sort of tracking process, but decided I was being paranoid and pushed on. I knew that one four one would be useless against a concerted effort, but I added it to the beginning of the number anyway.

The answer was near immediate, a foreign language, familiar, but not instantly recognisable. I hung on the line, holding my breath as more words came towards me. It took what felt like an age to hear the first phrase had been repeated, this time in English.

I'd got through to the Polish Embassy.

[Silence]

DD: And?

CH: I hung up the call. I remember the noise and bustle of the packed room had gone and as I turned, I expected all eyes to be pointed in my direction with the college guards striding toward me.

[Silence]

DD: But they weren't?

CH: No, of course not. The sound came back and I stood for a second, watching everyone absorbed in their roast dinner or conversations about what they were getting for Christmas, or what Susan said to Grace last night which meant they could no longer be friends.

I was the only one asking themselves why one of the lecturers had plans for a missile that wasn't in production. Why he was talking to a foreign power, albeit one that was expected to join NATO next year.

DD: Indeed.

CH: It was all I could think about all night. I managed a

45

couple of hours of sleep and in the end I was up by five and in the computer labs as they opened. I knew it was a risk, but I had to know if it was me being ridiculous; maybe the technology had just passed me by.

The only detail I could really remember about the piece of paper was the name on the top of the page, Project Chadwick. A quick search on Ask Jeeves came back with no definitive results, but what it did come back with turned my fears into a resolve. The only Chadwick linked to anything of significance was Sir James Chadwick.

DD: The Manhattan Project.

CH: Yes.

DD: But the Manhattan Project is history.

CH: But the implications for the missile designs were what peaked my fears.

DD: You thought it was related to a nuclear weapon.

CH: Yes, and I couldn't read anymore. What I thought was an act of espionage had now turned into something a whole lot more.

DD: Why didn't you just call the police or alert the authorities?

CH: I did. I wasn't going to report to the college. Who knew who was involved? I headed down to the village and made a call to the MET police.

DD: Why the MET and not the local police?

CH: The MET are responsible for co-ordinating anti-terrorism efforts across the UK.

DD: Okay. So why wasn't that the end of it?

CH: They didn't want to know. Well, whoever answered the phone didn't want to know. They asked me my age and details, but I refused to give them. They told me to go away and stop wasting their time as someone who really needed help could be trying to get through.

DD: How did that make you feel? Most people would have left it there.

CH: I felt annoyed. I felt belittled. I questioned myself, but only for a moment. By the time I got back to the college I'd decided that I would have to gather more evidence and nail this guy to the wall.

DD: That's a harsh attitude from a seventeen-year-old girl.

CH: Being seventeen and a girl didn't stop me wanting to make sure this guy didn't succeed. You of all people should know that people don't always fit in those neat little stereotypes society likes to build.

DD: Of course, you're right. So what was your plan to get more evidence?

CH: From that point on I decided to keep an eye on him, making efforts to happen to be where he was when I could. I'd organise myself so I wasn't out of place in the background and from those snapshots I'd build up his routine.

        In the morning he'd travel from his rooms on campus and have breakfast by himself, generally in the same seat. He'd eat alone nine times out of ten, and when one of the other staff joined him you could feel the discomfort pouring out. After breakfast he would head to the teaching complex, where he would teach back to back lessons, none of which I was in.

        He'd spend any free periods in the prep room and on a computer whose screen pointed out of the window of the second floor, facing out towards the south west spur of the building. Lunchtime he would dine with his peers; I got the feeling that if he could have got out of that he would have done, favouring a solitary life.

DD: Like yourself.

[Silence]

CH: He had the occasional visitor and I had to recruit some of my fellow students to help me out.

DD: You told them what you were doing?

CH: No, of course not. Most of these guys did fit into the stereotypes. I made up stories to cover why they were doing things, each only given specific tasks to complete, none of them knowing the real reason behind what they were doing.

DD: How did you get them to do what you wanted?

CH: My charms, of course.

[Silence]

CH: And chocolate.

DD: *[Laughter]* What sort of things would you tell them?

CH: I got one girl to trawl the internet for a history on Dubois, told her I had a crush on him and to find out if he had a family and a wife. I think she was more stunned that I'd expressed those sorts of feelings and that's why she just agreed to do it.

DD: You weren't into that sort of thing at the time?

CH: I was focused.

DD: Sure.

CH: But the end result came to very little. He was single, had a work history that was unremarkable, but included numerous defence contractors as his previous employers, which again was unsurprising for the college staff.

All this while, I kept up with my observations and trying not to let my work slip. In the evening he would spend an hour in the staff bar, but I couldn't get inside; no one I knew had been in. He would travel the short distance back to the flat, where he wouldn't be seen again till the morning.

Weekends were much the same. We'd have Saturday lessons, and PT on Sunday, but he was never involved. I was getting nowhere and on the verge of giving up. With no new suspicions I was beginning to talk myself out of the seriousness of what he was doing and if he was actually doing anything at all. I was close to putting it all down to my active imagination.

DD: I guess something must have happened?

CH: Yeah. I was working late on physics coursework with my group in one of the labs. I looked out of the window and I spotted the occasional flash of bright light from the main part of the Abbey across to the east. It was from the prep room.

Peering over, whilst trying not to raise suspicion, I could just make out the computer screen and a dark shape occasionally moving across it. I hurried to finish up, but the others wanted to continue so I told them I would call it a night. Instead of heading home, I blagged my way into the stores, giving some story about birdwatching in the morning.

The grounds were vast and set in an amazing estate. I grabbed a pair of binos and rushed back up to the labs. My group were still working away so I went to the next-door lab, which was in darkness, and rushed to the window. He was still at the screen.

SECRET – WHEN REDACTED

As I focused the glasses, I could tell straight away it was Dubois, his head bobbing rhythmically from side to side. No matter how I adjusted the binoculars, I couldn't see what was on the screen, but I could see he was copying and pasting something from one document to another.

I kept up my vigil for an hour, hoping to catch a glance. Either way, he wasn't doing anything normal.

The detail was elusive; no missile-shaped drawings, just lines of text and unfocused shapes, but as I first heard the clatter of activity down the corridor, I saw the logo for Matra BAe Dynamics heading one of the pages. Although he didn't seem to be finishing any time soon, I had to leave or risk having to explain to the cleaners what the hell I was doing.

Now I was sure he was up to no good; convinced he was stealing secret nuclear technology.

DD: So what did you do?

CH: I thought about going to the police again, or calling the Security Service direct, but I wasn't ready for another brush off. We were going home tomorrow. He was going to be leaving too and I was going to follow him.

DD: Uh?

CH: What?

DD: Sorry, nothing. I shouldn't interrupt. What did you tell your parents?

CH: I told them I'd be a few days late as I was going to stay with a friend.

DD: How did they react? Were they suspicious or worried you were going out of your schedule?

CH: They'd relaxed a bit since I'd joined the cadets and
        they thought I hadn't seen him in a long time. In fact,
        I was surprised when my mum seemed to be a little
        too happy for me. She said it was the first time I'd
        mentioned anything to do with any friends, but it
        didn't make me pause for long.
                The next day, after packing light, I waited
        close at hand, but I had no transport of my own, so
        when I saw his cab arrive and I overheard him tell the
        taxi to take him to the station I butted in, asking if I
        could share the ride. He wanted to tell me where to
        go, but in front of the driver he let me share.

DD: That must have been an awkward journey?

CH: Not really. I acted like some of the girls I bunked
        with, started rattling off loads of things I, they, were
        going to be doing over the break. He kept quiet and
        let me talk at him through the twenty-minute journey.
        All I managed to get out of him was that he was
        heading to London. He wouldn't even let me pay a
        share.

DD: I notice you didn't refer to any of your bunk mates as
        friends?

CH: Do you want to hear the rest?

DD: Please continue.

CH: At the station the timing was great, for him at least.
        The train was seconds from leaving as I followed him
        onto the platform, with only just enough time to
        hover before I could get on a few coaches down.
                I spent most of the journey either hiding
        from the conductor, only making myself known at
        the penultimate station, the rest of the time thinking
        about what the hell I was going to do when we
        actually got to wherever it was he was going.
                All of the questions cleared up of their own

accord. We arrived in London to a very busy Kings Cross station, which gave me ample room to slip into the crowd while keeping him in sight. The same trick with the cab wasn't going to work again, so I risked going up close as he got to the head of the line. I overheard him telling the driver he was going to the Hilton in Trafalgar and I jumped on to the tube, guessing the journey times should be about the same at that time of the day. That was until I realised I was being followed by two people.

DD: How do you know?

CH: I have this habit of taking in information, faces included.

DD: How do you do it?

CH: It's easy. All you need to do is pick something on each face you see and store it away.

DD: Like what?

CH: A mole, if you're really lucky, but maybe a set of thick eyebrows, or a slight kink to the nose. If there is nothing else to go on, then it's hair or an item of clothing. They can be changed, but sometimes it's the only option.

DD: In a railway station? There must be thousands of people.

CH: It works for me.

DD: The concentration required must be huge.

CH: Not really. It happens without me taking any active role.

[Silence]

DD: So what was it about these two?

CH: They were harder to spot. I now know why, of course, but one looked like he'd just stepped out of a barber, his short hair gelled in tiny spikes, his expression so neutral it had to be deliberate. The other had a slight point to both of his ears, instantly associating him with those logical aliens in Star Trek. I can't remember their names.

DD: Vulcans.

CH: I'll take your word for it. It was a bad one to choose, although it's not an active decision process. If the angle was wrong, I would have missed him. It's just what sticks out.

DD: I'm impressed.

CH: Don't be. As I said, it just happens. Anyway, I'd seen Ears hanging around the station and at the taxi rank, I now thought. Now both were on the same train, the same carriage as me. They weren't looking in my direction, weren't obvious about it, but at the time I was sure that when I stepped off the train I was going to be robbed.

DD: You're Hyper Vigilant, the most distinct case I've ever seen. Beware, it comes with a health warning. We need to talk about that at some point.

CH: Shall I continue?

DD: Please proceed.

CH: The tube was busy so it didn't look odd that I was standing by the doors. Out of the corner of my eye I could see one of them was further down the carriage, not quite as close to the doors as I was; the other was sitting down, pretending to read a newspaper.

        As the alarms chimed and the doors started to close, I jumped out of the train and without looking back, I left the platform and headed through the maze of corridors, jumping on the first train in the opposite direction.

I was still only two stations out from Trafalgar, so I ran the last mile, slowing as I was met with the bustle of the Square. I peered around the numerous places I could sit and watch the entrance to the hotel. First though, I headed to the reception desk, only to find there was no one of his name checked in, but I at least caught a glint of recognition in the receptionist's face as I described Dubois's pointed Gaulish features.

I left them scratching their heads and took up camp on a bench at the furthest point from the hotel and waited. It wasn't long before he was out again. He'd changed from the suit he always seemed to wear, into casual dark trousers and a jumper over his shirt. He carried no bags and seemed to have too few places to be able to hide anything of substance, like a file.

DD: Weren't you worried he would see you?

CH: He wasn't paying much attention to his surroundings. He wasn't doing any anti-surveillance, so I concluded he thought he was safe from anyone looking on.

Following him was easy in the crowds; it was a sunny Saturday and people were out Christmas shopping. I was able to vary my pace as the crowds built and thinned. It wasn't long before he turned into a pub just a few roads down from the square. I watched as he ordered a drink and as he pulled out his wallet, he slid the key card to the side to get at a ten-pound note. I continued to watch from the corner of the pub, peering over a snacks menu in my hand. He drank his pint slowly, craning up at the TV screen, occasionally looking around or at his watch.

He was waiting for someone.

That someone came. A bald someone, Slavic

looking, a someone who wasn't happy quite soon
after their conversation started. A someone who
looked around, searching for something, a bag or
folder I guessed.

Two guys joined my table, blocking my view
with pints of beer in their hands. They started
chatting to me, asking to buy me a drink, not hiding
their approaches. I tried ignoring them, but I knew I
was on rocky ground. I was seventeen and wasn't sure
how long it would be before I was asked to leave and
if I made a fuss, they could draw his attention. How
the hell would I explain that?

DD: How indeed?

CH: As they were talking, an idea came to me and I started
telling them I was spying on my stepdad. I told them
he beat me and my mum and that he was out drinking
with a friend and probably cheating on my mum, too.

I rolled up my sleeve and showed them a
dark purple bruise I'd got on the assault course only
a few days before. I said if they did something for me
then we could go somewhere else and I'd let them
buy me a drink. Their faces lit up and I felt like mine
did, too.

[Silence]

CH: Why are you making that face?

DD: No reason. Carry on.

CH: I just asked if they could discreetly steal his wallet. I
wanted the key card and they could keep what else
they found. I was surprised how they agreed in a flash
and I headed to the ladies to wait it out.

DD: Were they part of the challenge team?

CH: I don't know. The taller of the two joined me less
than five minutes later with a Cheshire cat smile and

the key card. I asked him if my stepdad knew about the wallet as I took the card and they said no; they left the wallet in place so he wouldn't know for a while.

A woman came in just at the right time and I stayed as he left in response to her rather indignant scowl. When the room was clear, I cat-crawled out through the window and into a small loading yard at the back and was soon in Trafalgar Square.

DD: You were lucky.

CH: Lucky how? That those guys came along?

DD: No, lucky you could get away. Do you realise the situation you could have gotten yourself into?

CH: I could handle myself. Anyway, the key card was a simple square of golden-coloured plastic, no markings of the room number, just the H of the hotel in italics in the centre. I headed up to the reception desk, making sure I wasn't speaking to the same guy who I'd already had words with.

I told them my uncle asked me to come down and inform them one of his keys wasn't working. The smiling receptionist took the key and asked me to confirm the room number. I leant over the desk and smiled, shrugging my shoulders. I just know it's up there, I said. I can ring him if you want? The guy smiled and I watched him tap 403 into the phone keypad.

As the phone rang out, I said he was just going into the shower and I would go back and get him to come down if he wanted, or ring down. The guy smiled back and gave me back the key, saying not to worry, but to come back down if I still had problems.

I was in and out of the room in seconds and under my coat was an A4 envelope full of a printed version of the files I'd seen on the screen. From the

56

briefest of looks, I could see the formatting was wrong, the headers and footers sometimes mingling with the main body of the text, but I still knew what it was.

DD: And what was it?

CH: A spec, a manual, a construction guide for a missile that no one had heard of unless they were in a very close circle.

DD: You're making a lot of assumptions. Just because a missile is in development, doesn't mean people don't know about it. I'm sure there will be an army of people in the defence world working on it.

CH: Yes, okay. But I knew by Dubois's actions he shouldn't have the file, or at the very least he certainly shouldn't be copying it and meeting some guy in a pub in London.

[Silence]

DD: Anyway, yes. We know that was meant to be the case now. Please, what happened next?

CH: As I left the hotel, I thought about running. I thought about addressing the envelope to Thames House and getting on with my Christmas. I knew that wouldn't be enough. I knew that would give them the chance of getting away with whatever they were doing. Dubois would disappear; the polish guy would melt back into the embassy.

        No, I had to act to get them both; they had to be found and detained now.

        I turned around and headed back to the hotel, borrowing a wedge of blank pages from the reception, stuffing them inside the envelope, replacing the important pages which I hid under my jacket. As I left the room for the second time, I passed

Dubois in the corridor, my head turned down at the floor. With a quick glance back, I could see he'd spotted his key card on the floor outside his door as he fumbled open his wallet.

I waited outside of the hotel, watching the entrance, watching the crowd, picking out possible faces I might have already seen too many times before. It was a long hour before he was back out, his right arm pressed to his side, the precious folder I guessed, as he walked stiff and indignant.

He strode right towards me; for a moment I thought I was spotted and was ready to run, but I stood my ground, my face turned away, my head buried in my hood. He passed right by my side and into the long queue for the National Gallery.

This was it. The exchange.

I made a call on the payphone just off the square and joined at the back of the queue. I was a comfortable ten places behind as the queue moved through the barriers. As I did, I heard a phone ring unseen and the barriers locked at my back, the end of the queue turned away.

He was easy to follow in the wide halls of the museum and with no surprise I soon saw the Polish guy from the pub stood at the end of a long hall, staring up at a tall portrait of a naval warrior. They stood side by side, but neither seemed to pay the other any attention.

I sat on a marble bench, it must have been ten metres back, but instead of taking in the giant portraits, I watched the two figures as they stared forward. The envelope was exchanged, their eyes still not meeting, their heads not turned, but gasps in the distance cut my stare short. The heavy stomp of feet made me stand; as the first armed officer appeared, the pair turned, somehow not noticing me. Both had drawn pistols.

Two shots rang out and the policeman was down, his gun spinning to my feet. His colleagues held back out of sight, the wall as their defence. The two turned and ran.

DD: What was going through your head at this time?

CH: Nothing, other than I couldn't let them get away. I just reached for the gun at my feet and I shot at the Polish guy with the folder. Two shots. No recoil. And I knew.

DD: Knew what?

CH: It was all an elaborate exercise. Dubois and the Polish guy pulled up from their run, turned back with their faces full of smiles and then walked away out of the room.

[Silence]

DD: How did you feel?

CH: I was trying not to process. I was trying not to think that I'd taken my first shot at a human being, albeit with blanks. Although I'd fired hundreds of rounds before, thousands probably, I'd never shot at someone. And all this was an exercise. I couldn't believe how someone could orchestrate this whole thing. The stuff at Welbeck, fine. But taking over the National Gallery and firing shots... I just didn't know how that could have happened.

DD: I guess it gave you an understanding of just how many resources and influence the organisation has.

CH: Not really, because at that stage I had no idea who was behind any of this. I just remember sitting back down, stunned as the realisation filtered through. The police officer got to his feet and those hidden at the wall melted away.

59

I was numb, my hand held out with the gun to the newly arrived figure. I remember his face was rough as bark and he offered his hand. He spoke my name, thanked me for all I'd done. He asked me question after question with a wide smile as I answered, my voice almost robotic in tone.

He complimented me over and over and told me I'd passed a test, passed the best anyone had before. Although I remember the words, my ears were full of cotton as I pulled the typed pages from under my coat. He told me the whole thing wasn't real, the pages were nothing but a fantasy. He told me I was now part of the team, if I wanted, that would protect the world; protect our way of life from harm.

DD: The tale lives up to the rumours.

CH: Rumours?

DD: Although it was only eighteen months ago, it didn't take long before the whole thing was buzzing around the community.

CH: What rumours?

DD: That there was someone coming up through the system who'd beaten the Chadwick Challenge. You're hailed as some sort of mega star, although only a few people know your real name or even what you look like.

You're like a modern-day Woodstock. Every other person who's heard of you will say they've met you on some operation or other. Most wouldn't think you're a woman, let alone not even operational yet.

CH: What do you think?

DD: I'm the wrong side of this table I'm afraid.

CH: *[Laughter]* They run the same challenge at Welbeck every year?

DD: Not just at Welbeck and not just in colleges. Sandhurst, and all manner of establishments and organisations. As you can imagine, the results vary wildly. You took it much further. You're the first to come home with the prize.

[Silence]

CH: Who else knows it's me?

DD: Only those with access to your files.

CH: Did you know?

DD: No. This goes way beyond me.

CH: The instructors?

DD: No, only a handful of people outside of the Chadwick operation.

[Silence]

DD: What gets me is your age. You were doing that the whole time most people your age were experimenting with life's new boundaries, putting one foot into adulthood.

CH: Instead I was following a fake foreign agent.

DD: *[Laughter]* Might as well have been real.

CH: Well some people don't have the introduction to life that I had.

[Silence]

DD: Do you want to expand?

CH: No.

DD: Okay. So from that, how did you end up here?

CH: We drove for an hour, towards my parent's house and

he explained that I should keep this all to myself, as impossible as that might seem in the moment. After the short holiday, I was to complete my time at Welbeck as if nothing had happened and continue on to Sandhurst. He told me which regiments to put down as my choice and said someone would be in contact and if I needed anything then he guessed I could figure out how to get in touch.

DD: This is extraordinary. So you went on to finish Welbeck, then Sandhurst? Do you want to take a break?

CH: No.

DD: What's troubling you?

[Silence]

CH: Do you think he is another extraordinary part of this process, or just my imagination?

DD: Nothing is impossible. If we're talking about your sightings long after the kidnappings. I have no doubt we were not involved in those.

     The times you were attacked were clearly very real. Witness reports and the police investigation cast no doubt, but it wouldn't be unusual for someone who had been through such a dramatic event to not have any after effects.

     It wasn't traumatic, but I lost my mother five years ago. I still catch a glimpse of her face on strangers and even though I know she's dead, I watch until they turn before I can look away.

CH: Do you want to talk about that?

DD: *[Laughter]* Very good.

CH: *[Laughter]* Sorry, and I am genuinely sorry for your loss. Sometimes it's like that for me too, but every so often he is actually there. Our eyes lock.

DD: Have you ever had flashbacks to either of the attacks?

CH: No. Dreams, yes, but at night and I don't wake covered in sweat. They're dreams.

DD: How is your mood generally?

CH: Flat. I'm a serious bitch all the time.

DD: Well you do a good job of hiding it.

[Silence]

DD: How's your sleep?

CH: I sleep like a log. You go through Sandhurst, or any military training where you're running your ass off sixteen hours a day and up at five each morning, you learn to sleep when you can. It's never been a problem for me. I could probably even get to sleep on this horrible plastic chair.

DD: Do you ever get woken by the dreams?

CH: No more than most. The dreams are nothing. It's not PTSD. I was screened before. It's just him.

DD: And no one else has ever seen him?

CH: No. I have only ever seen him when I'm alone and never in places where it was unlikely he would be there, like in college or on a Corp night.

[Silence]

CH: So why do you think my head would do this to me?

DD: Those two events had a huge bearing on your life and will have tempered every big decision you've made, even if you didn't realise it. You would have been watchful, waiting for the next time, but it didn't happen again. There was no release, no ending.

    The police investigation is unsolved, although I'm sure the case remains open. In short, it's that word that those in my profession tend to favour. You haven't had closure.

[Silence]

DD: Does this make sense?

CH: *[Laughter]* I tried to lay a trap for him once.

DD: Do tell.

CH: I must have been about fifteen, so I'd been out of gymnastics for nearly two years. I signed myself up to a local competition. I didn't want to go through ██████, who by now had became active as a volunteer in the Corp, as he would have quickly realised I had no thoughts of actually competing.

    I attended the event, but I didn't sign in. I was dressed very masculine, with a thick coat, my hair completely hidden in a baseball cap, my eyes behind thick rimmed glasses. I watched, but not the action on the mats. I watched everything else.

DD: And?

CH: He didn't turn up.

DD: What would you have done if you'd have seen him?

CH: I would have thought on my feet, called the police.

DD: Did you have the knife with you?

CH: Yes. For my protection.

DD: And if you had to protect yourself?

CH: I would do what needed to be done, but he didn't show up and I went home.

DD: Why do you think he didn't show?

CH: Maybe I didn't give him enough time to find the competition? Maybe he wasn't looking there anymore? Maybe I'd been out too long? Maybe he doesn't exist?

DD: Okay. Let's think about this. Why are you smiling?

CH: You're not sure, are you?

DD: I have come to no conclusion. How would he have known where you were, where you are, all this time?

CH: How did he know I would be at those two gymnastics events?

DD: Trawl the press? Is there a gymnastics monthly these things get published in?

CH: No press really. Not even a website back then. I guess it would have been word of mouth. Coach took care of all that for me.

DD: Did you ever see the guy around your house or where you lived?

CH: Not that I can recall. Sometimes I would properly see him as clear as I am seeing you, but not this close. Sometimes he would be in the corner of my eye. Sometimes I would see him and the person would turn and I would realise it wasn't him, like you said before. I know that is at least partly true.

DD: So again, how would he know where you were?

CH: Maybe he followed me from home.

DD: But you never saw him around your house?

CH: It was a busy area, on a main road. There were always people around.

DD: It would be almost impossible to keep tabs on you like that for such a long time. It would mean he wouldn't have a job. He'd need some sort of income.

CH: I didn't see him every day.

DD: How often?

CH: I can't really recall. I guess I would have what I call a confirmed sighting maybe every six or seven months, not that I was counting. I should have made a diary.

DD: Let's assume he knew where you lived. Let's assume his aim, for whatever reason, was still to kidnap you. Let's assume if he'd been keeping tabs on you for that long, why didn't he just take you at home?

CH: We were vigilant. The doors were always locked, self-locking. We had alarms, as I said before. Most of the time my mum was around. She didn't work; gave it up after the second attempt.

DD: On the way to and from school?

CH: Never alone.

DD: When you were out with your friends?

CH: What friends?

DD: You must have had some friends?

CH: I had gymnastics friends, but we were all training too hard to meet outside of the gym. When that came to its sudden end, I made friends at the Cadet Corp and that was where we socialised.

DD: You had no other friends? From school? Neighbours? Were you that much of an ugly duckling, repulsive to all who laid eyes on you?

[Silence]

66

DD: It's a two-way street. Give me something back.

[Silence]

CH: I wasn't disfigured, it was a choice. There were people I liked and that liked me. We would hang together in the playground, chat in school, but my mother was very protective. Between studying, gymnastics and the Cadet Corp, going on camps, walks and events, I had little time for much else. There were no mobile phones so no way to keep in touch other than through the home phone, and my parents kept strict control.

[Silence]

DD: What are you thinking?

CH: It's just that when I tended to get close to people, girls or boys, men or women, they tended to get a little intense.

DD: What do you mean?

CH: When I was in primary school, I used to have a load of friends. Well, they were friends with me, but not so close with each other. Some of them I'd become really close to. On several occasions I would have them over for tea, a normal everyday occurrence, but when the others found out, even though they had their own time around my house, they would get upset. Jealous, I guess. It was kind of a relief when we got our next posting to the other side of the country at the end of each third year.

DD: Did you keep in touch?

CH: No. No one wrote and neither did I.

DD: It ended, just like that?

[Silence]

DD: And you never made any more friends?

CH: In my last year of primary school it happened all over
       again. Without even trying I was getting close to this
       group of four friends, two boys and two girls. They
       were already good friends with each other, really
       close. Such nice guys. Then it started to get intense.

DD: How so?

CH: I don't really want to talk about it. When guys and
       sometimes girls get close, they want to take it too far.

DD: So you stopped getting close?

CH: Yes. I took away the opportunity from everyone.

DD: So you never went out? Never went to parties? Never
       did the things teenagers do?

CH: You mean normal teenagers?

DD: If you like.

CH: No. But I was, I am, fine with that.

DD: What did you do with your time?

CH: Read a lot, when my mum would let me out to the
       library.

DD: You like Stephen King?

CH: Yes. You?

DD: I don't get much time to read, but yes, I have read a
       few of his books. Which is your favourite?

CH: Carrie.

DD: Interesting choice.

[Silence]

DD: And when you weren't reading?

CH: I spent loads of time on AOL Instant Messenger.

DD: Chatting with friends from school?

CH: No. Strangers mostly, or people who I was friends with that had never actually met me. It didn't have the same problems. I remember those afternoons I would sit in front of the computer, listening to The Spice Girls and Tracey Chapman whilst scouring the twenty or so windows I would have open looking for the new message.

DD: So you never had a partner?

[Silence]

CH: No. I've never allowed anyone to get that close. I never let anyone get past the first barrier.

DD: What about gymnastics? The Corp? You said you socialised?

CH: I did. At the organised events. I was never alone with anyone for longer than I needed to be. I always turned down activities outside of the event. I always politely declined advances, for friendship or otherwise.

DD: And that worked?

CH: Yep. Everyone still wanted to be my friend, but I was the ice bitch with a nice smile. They all thought I was so busy with a jam packed schedule and I couldn't possibly fit in another morsel.

[Silence]

DD: But in reality you were going home to be locked inside a fortress with your parents.

CH: You make it sound like a Disney movie.

DD: All we need is a happy ending. Is there a happy ending?

69

CH: I'm living it.

DD: Do you hear how this comes across?

[Silence]

CH: If you're worried about how it affects my ability to lead others, it doesn't. I can inspire people when I want to and I can understand their motivations. You only have to look at my service record to date to see I do just fine.

DD: You don't think you come across as a border-line sociopath?

[Silence]

DD: Time for coffee, I think.

CH: You drink a lot of coffee.

Journal of Dr Devlin, Head of Occupational Psychology

Section A ███████████████

14th September 2000 - Session 1.3

Initial Opinions Cont'd

Ms H's actions in recruiting her fellow students, despite her aloofness, shows excellent leadership skills. She was able to positively manipulate others into doing what she needs, whilst covering up the true end goal.

Although I'd heard about the Chadwick Challenge and how it was used to find extraordinary individuals for the recruitment process, I was still amazed to hear Ms H's story. At seventeen she's following a college lecturer to London!

Ms H is clearly hyper-vigilant. Note to self to include in the risk assessment and monitoring matrix.

After hearing the details of the Chadwick Challenge, I can see more now how she could believe her stalker, certainly who he is now, not the original, could be part of the process. She has seen more effort in other areas put in by our employers, so it wouldn't be a leap.

Despite her assurances and I have confirmed she has been screened for PTSD, it cannot be ruled out, unless she is not holding back. I suspect this is not the case.

This issue with people getting close and taking it too far is very interesting, but I'm also respectful that she doesn't want to talk about it. It has little bearing on my report so I won't press too much for now.

She reacted well when I questioned her about her unwillingness to spend time with others and if she could be classed as a sociopath. She is right that her records from college and Sandhurst do show she is able to overcome this natural leaning. I believe as her environment changes for the positive, this could improve further.

The tell was there again when she spoke of coach .

TRANSCRIPT OF AUDIO RECORDING A1763529-1
[DEVICE C120 COVERT RECORDER]

[DATE:14ᵗʰ SEPT 2000] [15:00GMT]
[LOCATION: ▓▓▓▓▓▓▓▓▓▓▓▓▓▓▓▓ *]*

CH: Hi.

DD: Yes. Please sit.

CH: Thank you.

DD: So what about professional relationships? Teachers? Coach ▓▓? Staff at college? Sandhurst? Did you have trouble with them trying to get close?

CH: Not really. With other people, professional encounters I mean, it's easy to keep a distance.

DD: But people were still friendly?

CH: Yes. I guess they tried to get closer, but like I said, it was easier to keep my distance.

DD: So you shut everyone out?

[Silence]

CH: Sure, if you want to put it like that.

DD: Except Stacey?

CH: I guess so.

[Silence]

DD: I bet it was useful to be so likeable. To have people vying for your attention?

CH: Useful?

DD: It couldn't have harmed your progression, I mean.

CH: Sorry, are you trying to suggest that I won the Sword of Honour because I'm a likeable person? Are you

73

trying to say that I did anything but work my ass off to get to be the best in the year?

DD: No, not at all. No, no. I've seen your file and the citation from the Commandant says you would have been the best in any of the last five graduating years.

CH: Okay.

[Silence]

CH: Sorry.

DD: Fine. Let's change the subject. Do you think you missed out on your childhood?

CH: No. Well, other than nearly being kidnapped twice and having my dreams shattered, I don't think I did. I had, have, two loving parents and a fulfilled teenage life in the Cadet Corp and either a career in whatever this place is or in the Army, and you only have to flick onto the BBC News to see that it's going to be an interesting few years, whichever way this goes.

[Silence]

DD: So back to Evasion One. Fifty-four hasn't seen your man. Sorry, I'll rephrase that. She hasn't seen your…

CH: Call him what you like; stalker, imaginary friend. I've gone through the names so many times before.

DD: Let's stick with stalker for now. So when you turn your back he's not there?

CH: Correct and that's happened so many times before I didn't let it phase me. We went on to chat to the cafe owner, keen to get a lay of the land and get away from that place. We'd already been there too long and although unlikely, there was still a possibility we'd been tracked at least part of the way there.

        I told him we were passing through and

needed some work in the meantime. He mentioned the huge amount of casual work picking fruit on farms all over the country. I kicked myself for asking the stupid question and revealing our intentions.

It was harvest time so they're crying out for labour, most not even advertising in the local papers; everyone apparently knew about it. We decided to walk, which we did for a long while, not too worried about where we were going, just heading in the general direction away from the bright lights, and CCTV cameras, of outer Manchester.

About four hours later, we arrived in a place called Broadheath, using what could only be described as an indirect route, happy we would be difficult to find because we really had no idea where we were. With the little money we had left, we bought food and sat in a local pub and read through the local paper.

Despite what the guy said, we found promising ads and, with a few phone calls from the payphone on the corner, we'd identified three places we could just turn up to in the morning, the earlier the better and if they hadn't filled their slots, the jobs were ours for the day.

DD: So you planned to just work?

CH: We had a week to kill. We needed money for somewhere to stay.

[Silence]

CH: What would you have done?

DD: I have no idea, but that's not how this works. I'm making no judgement on your strategy, but the majority got hold of a tent and camped out.

CH: I'm not adverse to camping for a holiday or out on exercise, but if there's an alternative that lets you sleep in comfort and saves you from a diet of wild blackberries, I know which I'd take.

DD: But you could have just lost yourself in the countryside and lowered the risk of being caught?

CH: Where's the fun in that?

[Silence]

DD: Okay. What happened?

CH: Well, we still had the problem of where we were going to stay that night. We had less than thirty pounds left, plus the fake fifties, but they were too bad to consider unless we were desperate.

    Nursing drinks from the bar, we put off thoughts of sleeping under the stars in one of the fields just outside the little town. The landlord must have taken pity on us and brought over a free round. We got chatting. He was a young guy, seemed to be quite taken with Stacey. Why are you looking at me like that?

DD: It was just an involuntary raise of my eyebrow. I meant nothing by it.

[Silence]

CH: We mentioned our predicament. Told him that our hotel had fallen through and we'd paid over the phone, but didn't have any way of paying for the night a second time. They had rooms, the place was quiet, holidays were over, kids were all in school, everyone was back to the grind.

    All throughout he kept quiet, but I could tell he wanted to help. In the end, I just asked outright. I asked if he could give us a room for the night on trust and I would pay him double in a week's time. He didn't hesitate, told me to forget about the money and that his mum, the owner, was away, so they could have a room.

We needed to be out before six, but there was no way we would stay that long anyway. We took the room almost immediately, sleeping in our clothes in case we had to make a quick getaway.

DD: That should have been a safe place to stay. They shouldn't have known even what area you were in so I bet you slept well.

CH: Not bad, but there was always the possibility of being found. Maybe they'd tracked us to the drop off in Manchester. Maybe they had enough people to be able to ring around all of the hotels in the area and pass over our descriptions.

DD: Sounds unlikely.

[Silence]

CH: Well at four am there was a gentle knock at the door. At first I thought it was the guy coming to take payment. I remember the look in Stacey's eyes as we grabbed our packs, ready to run, checking outside and down the sheer drop to make sure there wasn't a line of hunters with cages ready for us.

It was the manager, the same guy as before, but we knew by his demeanour we'd been wrong about him. He explained that he'd woken to pee and saw a message on his phone from the night manager, asking what happened to the two women he'd been speaking to.

The police wanted to speak with us urgently. The night manager had given the details. That was an hour before. There was no decision to be made; he held the door as we paced down the corridor, through the bar and into the kitchen where we headed out of the back door.

DD: Why do you think he helped you?

77

CH: I asked as we were leaving. He said he didn't believe
        we were capable of doing anything bad.

DD: A good Samaritan. That's refreshing.

[Silence]

DD: Why the big smile?

CH: I'm just remembering the look on his face when I
        planted a grateful kiss on his lips.

[Silence]

DD: And you ran?

[Silence]

DD: There's that smile again.

CH: Not straight away. Why are you so surprised?

DD: Again, not the way this works. I'm just a little taken
        aback that you didn't get out of there when you could.

CH: Never play poker.

DD: It's a strategy to get you to relax.

CH: *[Laughter]* There was valuable intel on offer so I
        couldn't pass it up. I split with Stacey, setting up a
        meeting point and a time period. If we weren't able
        to meet up then I told her to go it alone.

DD: Why did you split?

CH: I knew what I was going to do had some risk. It had
        been my decision, my idea. I didn't want her getting
        caught if something went wrong.

DD: You're blushing.

CH: I don't blush.

DD: I don't have a mirror, so you'll have to take my word for it.

CH: It's just, as we said goodbye, she pecked me on the lips.

[Silence]

CH: It took me by surprise, that's all.

[Silence]

CH: Can I ask what you're writing about? It was nothing, just a friendly gesture. We'd been through a lot together in the last twenty-four hours.

DD: Please don't take any inference from what I do, or when I make a note or what facial expressions I may form and even from the words I say. I am not here to judge; I am here to record and bring out information. That is all.

CH: Okay. Okay. Sorry.

DD: Please continue.

CH: I watched her vanish into the darkness in the opposite direction.

DD: How did that make you feel?

CH: There was a pang of guilt for letting her go off on her own, but a little relief, too.

DD: Relief that you didn't have to carry her anymore? Guilt that she wouldn't last without you?

CH: I wouldn't say that. Well, maybe a little. More of a thought that I didn't have to run everything by someone else. I could make my own decisions.

DD: You work better on your own?

CH: Maybe, but I definitely work differently when I'm in a group. Anyway, I watched her head off in the direction we'd agreed, the opposite heading from our meeting point in case we were being watched. As she disappeared, I took up my place in a shop doorway just across from the pub entrance.

The entrance was in shadow and the wheelie bins were out on the street for collection, so at least I had something to hide behind when the sun came up. I waited there, but it wasn't long before I heard a large engine car coming down the street.

In fact, it was two X5s with blacked-out windows, the whole cliché. They pulled up directly outside the hotel, a guy and girl jumping excitedly from each. I took a moment, absorbing what I could from their uninteresting features lit just enough in the dawning light, each of them dressed as casual as if they were strolling to get the Sunday papers.

I was confident they couldn't see me even if they had bothered to take a moment to look around, and I watched them disappear through the opening pub door as the car's central locking snapped into place and the lights flashed twice.

I'd got what I'd come for; their appearance was as expected, descriptions that would fit half of the population, their vehicles the same, knowing their tactics were lazy, their focus somewhere else. As I was about to sneak from my position, I heard what I thought was another car, another X5, I was sure, but soon there was something else, something bigger.

DD: The bin lorry?

CH: You got it. An X5 too, again in black, the perfect match. The index was only three digits different. Sometimes you don't have to make it that easy.

DD: I'll pass on the feedback.

CH: It parked right next to me, making me crouch tight behind the bin, all the while the sky lightening. Out jump two more greys, nearly running as they headed to the back door.

DD: Greys?

CH: Grey operators. Nothing men. Blending into the crowd kind of people.

DD: Okay.

CH: I remember them, instructors this time, on the periphery; well, at the least the driver anyway. He'd led some of the hikes and PT. Bit of a twat, if I remember rightly.

[Silence]

CH: He's not going to see this is he?

DD: No, no. No one gets to see the details of what you tell me, just what's in my summary report.

CH: Yeah, well, as I said, he was up himself. Voice of a toff, but the manners of a monkey. Kept on spitting everywhere whenever he built up a sweat. Some problem, I guess.

       Anyway, something made me pause as I stood. I hadn't heard the click of the locks; the lights didn't flash. I looked up and down the street. The bin lorry's engine note had changed and I could feel my face highlighted by the sun burning over the horizon beyond the hotel. A scurry of fluorescent jackets pulled up the bins; it was now or never to make a break.

DD: And so you ran off to meet with Stacey and tell her about the positive sighting.

CH: No.

DD: This time I guessed as much.

CH: The next thing I know, I have my fingers on the handle of the X5's back door. It's only when I was pulling I realised there could be anything, or anyone, beyond the blacked-out windows. Still I pulled.

A simple black kit bag sat on the leather, its zip half open. I pushed my hand in and a male aroma spilled up as I rooted around, drawing out a small leather folder. I glanced up to the room we'd been in only minutes before and with the all clear I opened the folder to find a plain page of typed writing, a short list, rules of engagement.

I didn't read it; instead, I pulled a wad from a bunch of fifty-pound notes lining the left of the pouch and although I didn't pause to check, they looked and felt as real as I'd ever seen before. To the right, in the staggered leather slots were ID passes, each with the same face, the same name; the only differences were the badges of the official government organisations.

I left them in situ, but as I placed the pouch back in the bag, I felt a thin length of material brush against my hand. I couldn't help smiling as I pulled out the pass on the lanyard and pushed the door back into place. I was into the nearest alley a moment later and away down a maze of paths cut into the hill. I kept an eye on my back, but by the time I saw two of the X5s snaking away along the road, I would have just been a pin prick.

DD: That was very brave of you.

CH: It didn't feel like it at the time.

DD: Weren't you worried about being caught?

CH: It was an assessed risk.

DD: So you did think about it?

CH: Of course. When I was away, my thoughts turned to

what I'd just done and how close I could have come to getting caught. It would have only taken for someone to have been behind the blacked-out glass, or for one of the hunters to rush around the corner and that would have been it.

It was all I could think about as I made my way to meet up with Stacey. If anyone had come near me, they would have thought I was insane, I was laughing so much to myself.

DD: Laughing?

CH: It was either that or cry.

DD: When did you last cry?

CH: Really? Are you asking that?

DD: No. We'll get to that later.

[Silence]

CH: The guy from the hotel, he did us a good turn and I'm so grateful.

DD: He aided and abetted a wanted criminal.

CH: It's all about perspective.

[Silence]

DD: Yes. That's what he thought he was doing. How do you feel about using your sexuality to get what you want?

CH: I didn't.

DD: If you were a man, or a fat, balding woman, alone with just your glowing personality, do you think he would have done the same?

CH: Stacey was there, too. She was the one flashing her teeth and chest in his direction.

DD: But my guess is he was just talking to you. You were the one he offered the room.

[Silence]

DD: What about those men in the pub? The ones who stole the key card for you. Do you think they would have done that if you were a seventeen-year-old boy, or if you looked like the back of a bus?

CH: I really don't do that.

[Silence]

CH: Do I?

DD: You're doing it now.

CH: What?

DD: Curling your hair in your fingers, subtly pouting your lips.

CH: I'm not.

DD: Your posture is practically inviting me to look at your chest.

CH: Well I hope you enjoy the lines of my grey sweat top.

[Silence]

CH: Have you ever thought that maybe *you* see what you want to see?

DD: To some extent you're right, but it's me on this side of the table. Please answer the question.

[Silence]

CH: I didn't think I did. I get on with people. I'm very personable.

[Silence]

CH: I get on well with both sexes.

DD: Do you think it's all down to your sunny personality?

CH: What do you mean?

DD: Don't be coy now. You're a very attractive woman. I'm sure you've been told that many times.

CH: Not really. I'm one of the lads. Since joining the Cadet Corp I'm more of a tom boy. I don't wear make-up. I only wear a skirt when I'm forced into uniform.

DD: So how would you feel if you were to start using your sexuality?

CH: I wouldn't know how.

DD: Okay, let's approach from a different angle. Are you a virgin?

CH: Do I really need to answer that question?

DD: I'm sorry if some of my questions make you feel uncomfortable, but I need to make a full evaluation, and if you are honest with yourself you will understand that I am helping you. I can get a female member of staff to take over if you prefer?

[Silence]

CH: Do you mean have I ever had sex?

DD: Yes.

CH: No.

DD: Have you ever been intimate with a man?

CH: Describe intimate.

DD: You can't make me feel uncomfortable.

[Silence]

DD: I mean fooling around, kissing, a grope, touching your vagina, your breasts, making you orgasm, either clitoral or through penetration.

CH: No. Or with a woman before you ask and yes, I have masturbated, to head that one off.

DD: These are standard clinical questions and I derive no embarrassment from them and neither should you.

CH: I haven't, but is this going to be a problem? Do I have to nip out and lose my cherry so I can be selected?

DD: Of course not. That idea is absurd.

[Silence]

DD: Do you find men attractive?

CH: Are you asking for a friend?

DD: Miss Hughes.

CH: Sorry. Yes, I find men attractive.

DD: Do you find women attractive?

CH: In what way? The female form can be a beautiful thing, I think most men and women will agree.

DD: I am not judging. Do you find women sexually attractive?

CH: Do you?

DD: I am not the one on that side of the process, but no.

[Silence]

CH: I do.

DD: Thank you. Please remember to try and not make any inference from my taking notes at this point.

86

CH: I'll try.

DD: Back to Evasion. What happened next?

CH: I met with Stacey. I was very late, about two hours after the deadline, but she was still there. I didn't have sex with her, before you ask.

DD: Miss Hughes, please.

CH: Sorry. I counted the cash. They had non-consecutive serial numbers and neither of us could find any flaws in the time it took for me to explain what had happened. We had a haul of five hundred pounds, which was more than enough to get us hotels for the rest of the week.

        We made our way south, just heading in the vague direction, using a map to point towards any town or villages. After five hours we arrived in Macclesfield, pretty confident our pursuers wouldn't be able to ring around all of the hotels in the north west. Still we went in separately, Stacey doing the paperwork, with me following after.

        We stayed in the room, ate room service and watched crap TV. We were out of there by seven in the morning and into Macclesfield town to stock up on new clothes and a few essentials, including a wig for me.

        It wasn't until the next day, after a good night's sleep right on the outskirts of Stoke on Trent, that we found they were upping the pressure. Passing a newsagent, we saw the headline on the board outside. Something like, 'Two Escaped Murderous Women on the loose'.

        Stacey grabbed the paper and with all of the local sheets carrying a similar headline and description that easily fitted us, you can imagine what went with it: 'Dangerous. Do not approach,' along with the number of a hotline to the local incident room. We were thankful they weren't able to display our photos and ruin our cover for whatever this job is going to be, but still we were watching over our shoulders even more and it put pay to the easy life we'd had since Broadheath.

The descriptions turned out to be easy to defeat, even with just a brunette wig; I was loathed to cut my hair if I could have avoided it, but Stacey chopped her blonde to a bob and dyed it black.

DD: I'm surprised you were loathed to cut your hair. I thought you were more of a tomboy?

CH: Growing up yes more so. Still, like I said before, I'm barely in a dress or skirt but I do love my hair.

[Silence]

CH: Even the clothes we were wearing were a match for the description, so wigged up we changed as soon as possible. Still with three days to go, the only other change we could make was to split up. And that's what we did. I gave her half the money and told her I would see her in the lecture theatre on Sunday and went our separate ways.

DD: Did you think about calling a tip off?

CH: For Stacey? No.

DD: What's different between the five guys you let be captured when you planted the phone?

CH: You say I let them get captured, but they had their own phones. I just ditched mine to make sure I wasn't being singled out. I guess neither of us know if it was their phones, my phone or their own mistakes that got them captured so early. Unless you know something operationally that you're not mentioning?

[Silence]

88

CH: Anyway, calling in Stacey would only serve them with more intel, give them my approximate location and confirm I was now travelling alone.

DD: Were you worried that if they found her, which they did only the next day, she would tell them about your plans?

CH: No.

DD: How could you be so sure?

CH: We'd been through a lot together and I know her so well.

[Silence]

CH: Anyway, she didn't know my plans.

DD: How well do you know her?

CH: Ah. You're picking up this thread. *[Laughter]*

[Silence]

CH: We were at Sandhurst together. Eventually we were in the same company, Normandy. I picked up an injury and left the course for a term. When I came back Stacey was joining the same company I'd been reallocated to. She was back-termed twice from Intermediate division; she'd been in Lucknow Platoon, recovering from an injured ankle for a year. She helped me settle in.

DD: I see you were lucky, too. You had your appendix out while you were on medical leave.

CH: Yeah, lucky me. I almost didn't get back in; they nearly had me off for another term to recuperate.

[Silence]

DD: You were the youngest on the course. That must have

been difficult.

CH: Not really. I was physically strong. I had no issue with the academic stuff. It may have been a problem if I hadn't kept myself to myself. The company I had started with were a whole term ahead of me; Normandy had already bonded together for three months.

DD: And you were the only one of the normal intake to go through without a degree. That must have been difficult.

CH: Yes. I went straight out of Welbeck. A decision not too favourable with the Commandant, I understand, but that soon quietened down as I seemed to be handling the course.

DD: *[Laughter]* Handling the course. Very Good. And Stacey helped?

CH: Yes. She helped me in spite of my coldness. In the end I thawed.

DD: What made you change?

CH: She was relentless, but not like the others had been in the past. She just seemed to care and didn't want anything from me.

[Silence]

DD: It must have been hard to sit out a whole term.

CH: Yes, especially as it was just a niggle, but they knew my history and didn't want to risk it. I kept occupied to fend off the frustration.

DD: What did you do while you were away?

CH: Watched bad TV for the most part.

DD: I can't seem to find any notes from the medics.

CH: It was just a niggle, as I said.

[Silence]

CH: Anyway, after a while I opened up, to her at least, and we became good friends.

DD: So what do you know about her?

CH: She's twenty-three. She's the first in the family to go to university and the first to go to Sandhurst. Back-terming took a bit of a toll on her, but she was okay.

DD: Where does she come from?

CH: Norfolk, I believe.

[Silence]

CH: So did she squeal?

DD: I wouldn't know and wouldn't tell either. The result, I guess, should speak for itself, which leads us to the next part of the story I'm keen to hear. Did you have much more trouble after Stacey left you?

CH: No, but I was more careful with my story, bought a suitcase and a blouse in a charity shop, looked business-like when I checked into hotels. With Stacey not by my side and the adjustments to my look I was now a million miles from the description. So I stayed in comfort with time to prepare for my return.

DD: Ah, yes, the part where you are to be back at HQ without getting caught. I believe there was a truck out on the perimeter road you had to get to in order to claim one of the winner's positions.

CH: The actual objective was to be in the lecture theatre by the deadline without having been caught.

DD: That's not what I heard.

CH: His exact words were, 'There will be a truck parked outside the northern entrance gates, departing at 10:00. Those on the truck by the deadline will receive immunity from capture. Those who do not start the course proper at 11:00 in this lecture theatre will have failed and take no further part in the process'.

DD: So why not just get to the truck?

CH: I didn't want one of the winner's positions. I wanted the winner's position, so I'd already abandoned that course of action.

DD: Indeed. I remember sitting at the head of the table on the rostrum in the lecture theatre. All but those who'd made it to the truck were sat down. I remember the cleaner clearing up a mess of water someone had spilled, the look on the CAPOPs face when he had to start with the floor still being mopped.
        Everyone looked clean and rested, if not a little stern. The door opens and in walked the rag tag bunch of five that had made it to the truck. They repeated the count twice before confirming you were the only one missing. The CAPOP seemed rather smug. Now what did he say?

CH: He said, 'At least most of you survived in one piece. Congratulations to the five of your colleagues who have made it back undetected. The rest of you need to up your game to get through this process.'

DD: And then you said?

CH: 'Six, sir,' as I pulled the wig off and carried on mopping the floor.

DD: I shouldn't smile, but the look on everyone's face was a picture, especially the CAPOP's. He looked like he was going to explode. You were lucky you were in the winner's group when they separated you.

CH: Yes, the grilling I got was worth it.

DD: So how did you penetrate this high security facility?

CH: Sad to say, but it wasn't too difficult. I made a few calls and found a key piece of information. I had to wait until one of the guys, and no I'm not giving any names away, was on shift at Sandhurst. He was more than willing to help me along, knowing it was for a good reason and he wouldn't be implicated.

DD: What did you find out?

CH: The route the laundry delivery takes.

DD: The laundry? How did you know it's not done in-house?

CH: Little marks, initials in the corner of all the towels. I noticed them when I dropped my kit in my room before Evasion.

DD: So how did you know Sandhurst would be able to tell you where we get our laundry done?

CH: My Sandhurst guy didn't and I didn't ask him. I simply asked him to find out where the Infantry Battle School got their laundry done and when it was delivered.

DD: You've lost me.

CH: One of the towels must have been mixed up. It had different markings to all those in my room. I guessed it was a shared contract because IBS is just down the road.

DD: I didn't know that.

CH: Now I knew the day of the week for the drop off, a Saturday for my luck, then it was easy to find the laundry itself. Rifling through the driver's paperwork told me this place was the second stop, and I had a reasonable idea of where this place was, based on the travel time to drop us for Evasion.

Getting in the lorry was easy; you guys get through a lot of sheets and kit. I just had to wait to be dropped off.

Getting off was a little trickier. In the end, I hid in one of the sacks. I got battered around a little, but once back inside, the pass I got from that instructor gave me a free run of the place. I spent the night in my own quarters.

DD: Your own quarters? *[Laughter]*

CH: I think that was the CAPOP's favourite bit. I snuck into the lecture theatre in the cleaner's gear using a cut down version of my wig, threw a load of water on the floor, put out the signs and the rest you know.

DD: Why is it you seem to have the knack for the Evasion exercise?

CH: It was common sense. Don't plan. If you do, don't write it down and don't tell anyone. Don't contact anyone you know, they can all be tracked. No phones, no tricks, don't come up for air. Stay out of the cities and they don't have a chance of finding you.

DD: So you knew you were taking unnecessary risks and breaking your own rules?

CH: Yes.

DD: Do you think that's because it was a simulated situation?

CH: It felt pretty real at the time, but I knew nothing worse than a dressing down was at the end if I got caught.

DD: And if it was real?

CH: I have no idea. I can only guess.

DD: Where did he put you in the rankings?

CH: CAPOP told me I was sixth because I'd not got to the truck, but one of the other instructors took me aside and told me I'd been put at the top, above the other five.

[Silence]

CH: I hope Instructor Davies doesn't get in too much trouble.

DD: I'm afraid he's been moved on. You highlighted a major security fuck up, let alone the fact he didn't report the loss of his pass. Somehow, he got away with not having it for a couple of days. But don't feel bad, it's been the catalyst for a number of important changes.

CH: I don't.

[Silence]

DD: Did you get a rest for a few days before you moved to the next phase?

CH: *[Laughter]* I was barely out of the debrief before they were putting us through our paces with a ten-mile hike piled with field kit.

DD: Those of you that remained.

CH: Yes. We were down to the low forties already by then; we'd just lost another five culled after the week's physical.

DD: What's next?

CH: You tell me, but it starts in ten minutes.

Journal of Dr Devlin, Head of Occupational Psychology

Section A ████████████

14th September 2000 - Session 1.4

<u>Initial Opinions Cont'd</u>

Ms H is starting to open up in this session and has shown a lighter side of her character. She is also showing she has a bravery which is only matched by her ambition to succeed. However, sometimes she does seem to worry herself with the things she does and maybe not thinking them through, like when she pulled open the car door, only then worrying there may still be someone in the back.

She seems very naïve or confused about her relationship to Stacey. She brought up the peck on the lips and then seemed to get embarrassed about having spoken about it. From the little I have seen, this is one of her first emotional reactions and she brought it up by herself.

Despite any feelings she may or may not have toward Stacey, she reasonably freely admits that she likes to operate on her own. This needs to be explored more.

There is some concern she is helping candidate Stacey (54) get through the process, however I will not interfere outside of my remit.

Ms H describes herself as personable and when she mentioned this it caused me to think. Her answers to questioning and the stories she recounts are at odds with this characterisation, however in person she is indeed pleasant to be around and I find myself agreeing with her that she is personable. I am left wondering which is the true case. It is unlikely she is both, so either she is giving an altered account of her actions, either deliberate or not, or she is an excellent actress.

Although Ms H's attitude is relaxing as the session goes on, I'm surprised as someone who has just gone through Sandhurst with flying colours that she's not more regimented in how she talks to me. Not being a military officer could be part of that, but if appropriate I will try and explore this further.

She has a definite drive to try and succeed as shown in her want to be in the lecture theatre rather than on the truck like everyone else. At first, I thought she was taking a huge risk that she'd be disqualified, but it would appear she carefully considered the rules, if not the spirit of the exercise. There are certain instructors who believe this was a great victory, but there are others who don't believe she should have gotten away with what they consider to be breaking the spirit of the rules.

There is much to explore if she makes it into later sessions. I have every confidence that I will be seeing Ms H again. On reflection of the conversations, I'm mindful that we mostly talk about the negative aspects of Ms H's past. I will look to address this if we have more sessions.

TRANSCRIPT OF AUDIO RECORDING A1763529-1
[DEVICE C120 COVERT RECORDER]

[DATE:16th SEPT 2000] [13:00GMT]
[LOCATION: ███████████████████████ *]*

DD: Take a seat. Sorry for calling you in so soon after our last meeting.

CH: It's fine. It's warm in here at least.

DD: I'll get straight to it as I know I'm taking up valuable time. After our meeting a couple of days ago, I was left with an unease that I'd missed something important and I wanted to have a quick chat.
        Each time we spoke about your coach, ████████ ████, you would give a tell. I made notes of it each time. A shuffle in your seat, or a movement, almost as predictable as the ticking of the clock.

[Silence]

DD: You just did it again.

[Silence]

DD: What is it about ████████ ████ that causes such a physical response?

[Silence]

DD: Did you have a relationship with him? I mean, a relationship that was inappropriate for your age?

CH: No.

DD: Okay. Well what is it then?

CH: He died.

[Silence]

DD: I'm sorry to hear that.

[Silence]

DD: You looked up to him.

CH: Yes. He dragged me out of the hole and got me on this path. I have a lot to be grateful to him for.

DD: Why do you think you have such a physical reaction to his name being mentioned?

[Silence]

CH: I don't know. Maybe I haven't quite dealt with his death yet.

DD: How did he die?

[Silence]

CH: He went off on some course and never came back.

DD: Was he operational?

CH: For who?

DD: Armed Forces? Our friends on the river?

CH: I was fifteen. I have no idea. He told me he was off on a course; I saw him after around three months when he checked in on a Corp night. He looked great, seemed to be well. Another three or four months went by and word came back that he'd passed away.

DD: But no idea how?

CH: Supposed to be a weakness in his heart.

DD: But you didn't believe it?

CH: I was fifteen. He was my hero. I didn't want to believe he was vulnerable.

DD: I'm sorry.

CH: It's not your fault.

DD: I think I have everything I need. Thank you, Miss
        Hughes.

Journal of Dr Devlin, Head of Occupational Psychology

Section A ███████████

16th September 2000 - Session 2

The death of Coach █████ ████ has clearly hit Ms H hard and it is an area which will need exploring as time goes by. I feel the ticks are a sign of her unresolved issues.

TRANSCRIPT OF AUDIO RECORDING A1763529-1
[DEVICE C120 COVERT RECORDER]

[DATE:1ˢᵗ NOV 2000] [14:00GMT]
[LOCATION: ▮▮▮▮▮▮▮▮▮▮▮▮▮▮▮▮▮▮▮ *]*

DD: Hello Miss Hughes, take a seat.

CH: You've not managed to get any potted plants yet then? Why are you looking at me like that?

DD: I'm sorry. It's just you look so different. Your eye. How did you do that?

[Silence]

CH: Oh, it was a couple of days ago. A training accident, that's all.

DD: Do you want to talk about it?

CH: I don't need to talk about it. Do you?

DD: Of course not.

[Silence]

DD: Are you coping okay? If you don't mind me saying, you look like they've been putting you through the mill.

CH: I look like shit, I know, but I'm coping about as well as the others, I expect. The physical stuff and the sleep routine is tough, but it's kind of reminiscent of Sandhurst. The Spec Ops guys are taking it in their stride of course, marking themselves out like beacons.

DD: Yes, they've been through worse, believe me. So how many candidates are we down to now?

CH: Well, it's been over a month now since out last chat.

[Silence]

CH: We've lost four with injuries during the physical training; everyone left seems to be coping with the physical strain at least. We had three dropouts recently, one after the other. I don't think they quite realised what a shit shower they were getting into, if you excuse my language.

DD: Of course.

[Silence]

DD: What was that look for?

CH: What look?

DD: The raise of your eyebrows.

CH: It was just your reaction to me saying shit shower. Sorry if you think I sound like a man sometimes.

DD: I don't want to come across sexist.

CH: But you think it is unbecoming of a woman?

DD: No. Just unexpected from a young female officer in the Army.

[Silence]

CH: Have you ever been in a barracks? Even a female one?

DD: No.

CH: I suggest you don't then. You'll hear much worse.

DD: Indeed. We were talking about the dropouts.

CH: Yes.

[Silence]

CH: Another handful will be going soon, I guess; there's a few wavering. Two guys fell asleep on their continuous surveillance stint a couple of nights ago and they went immediately. More and more have been leaving over the recent weeks because we're into suitability testing. Some people just aren't cut out to do what we're being asked. Not that anyone knows what we're really going to be asked to do, and for whom.

DD: At least no one's died yet.

[Silence]

DD: Don't forget the whole process started at five hundred before you all got together here. Do you ever discuss who could be sponsoring this project?

CH: Not really. I think everyone assumes it's the government in one form or another. Anyway, it's one of the clauses of the contract we signed. No one wants to risk losing their wages for saying the wrong thing.

DD: How are the remainder coping with the ever-shrinking size of the cohort?

CH: There's an underlying tension in the group, although I think that's deliberate. Working hard nineteen hours a day, sleeping on five hours will do that, I guess.

DD: Do you have any concerns?

CH: Only that I get injured, but that's mostly out of my control.

DD: How's the ankle?

CH: It's fine. I'm fine. It would just be the worst way to leave.

[Silence]

DD: So how are you getting on with the instructors?

CH: Getting on? Just great.

DD: Why don't I believe you?

CH: They wake us randomly in the middle of the night or just as we go to sleep to make sure we're not too rested. Every couple of weeks or so, randomly it would seem, they'll put a hood over your head and march you in the dark somewhere. We have no idea where because they walk you around in a circle until your head swims and you lose all sense of direction.
          You'll be forced into a seat and the hood will be pulled off. You'll be in this tiny interview room, two instructors sat opposite, different each time and they'll ask you stupid questions about your background, your life before the process.

DD: What kind of things would they ask you?

CH: What you would do in different situations. Sometimes they'll be nice, other times not so. If the answer is not what they think is fitting then you get screamed at. It's weird because sometimes you get the idea that they're on your side; I mean of all of the candidates.

[Silence]

CH: They seem to will us on, trying to motivate us on that last mile of the hill climb or the swim in the freezing open water. The next time you see them they'll be screaming at you for getting something wrong.

DD: Keeps you on your toes, but you're all smiles.

CH: That's because sitting here is the most relaxation I've had for weeks.

DD: I'm glad I can help. So no favouritism them?

CH: *[Laughter]* No. That stuff we spoke about the first time we met, it's out of the window here. I'm getting treated just as badly as the other candidates.

105

DD: So tell me about the instructors?

CH: Don't you know them?

DD: Of course I do. This is just part of an exercise. Please just give me your assessment of the instructors.

CH: Assessment?

[Silence]

CH: Is this feedback time? Do you have a cardboard slip for me to circle smiling faces to show my satisfaction, or do I score them on a one to ten basis, one for I'd invite them into my bed to be my first or ten for they haven't quite killed me yet?

DD: You seem upset.

CH: No, sorry, just tired. I don't really care what we talk about, as long as I can get another coffee.

[Silence]

CH: Thank you.

DD: You're welcome.

[Silence]

CH: That's good stuff.

[Silence]

CH: They don't tell us their names, but I've had plenty of time with my own thoughts.

[Silence]

DD: It always surprises me that they don't share code names with the candidates. I guess it's to avoid familiarity. Tell me your thoughts, please.

CH: Okay. I'm sure you can play along and see who you

recognise.

[Silence]

CH: You wouldn't be raising your eyebrows if you've had the few weeks I've had.

DD: Go ahead.

CH: There's Archie. He's just below average height, built too big to be on active service, despite what he says. Those muscles would get in the way and they make him stick out, but he definitely has that confidence. He's pretty average in my opinion. Likes to work you hard, tends to be in the Land Rover though, rather than running alongside.

DD: I don't know an Archie?

CH: Arch Bish.

DD: Very good. Desmond Tutu again.

CH: Yes, and he has a twin sister, Mel. Same build, average height.

DD: I don't think I want to know.

CH: Women can't be in spec ops, but she clearly wants to be. Go on, don't think too much about it.

DD: Ah, Wannabe.

CH: That's it. You know the Spice Girls?

[Silence]

CH: She wants more than anything else to be in the SAS. *[Laughter]* She's too big to run and talks like a man, just an octave higher. She's a mirror image of Archie in every way. Then there's one that looks like a lawyer, although I could be less kind.

          A lot of them are your classic 'grey man,' but

he is the deepest shade. If he stood still for too long, he'd fade into the walls, like a chameleon. Suddenly he'll move and you'll catch him out of the corner of your eye. I still can't get used it. Haven't really had many dealings with him; he seems quite quiet.

Oh, yes, and there's Tom. Of course, I have no idea what his real name is but, if you close one eye, squint through the other when it's dark and you're just out of focal distance, he has an uncanny resemblance to Tom Cruise. You know the one out of *Mission Impossible.*

DD: I am familiar with the film.

CH: Anyway, he's kind of nice, probably the most friendly out of them all, not that he's a chatterbox. If you had a box of scorpions you had to put your hand in, they're all going to sting you, but it's like he's not going to sting you quite as much. Despite that, he's still a scorpion.

You understand what I mean?

DD: Yes.

CH: Then there's the advanced driving instructors. I spent fourteen hours with one of the traffic Hitlers. Sorry, that's a little unkind. We were dropped off in Bristol, two of us together. We met a guy with grey hair, but with a jet-black moustache that was a little too small above his lip. Do you know what I mean?

Perhaps I didn't get along with him because he kept telling me off for not noticing something on our assessment. I had to drive up to Aberdeen as fast as I could whilst giving constant commentary as if we were in a car pursuit. I did it in just under seven hours. He wouldn't let me sleep on the return. Instead, he made me point out everything the next guy missed as we drove back on the opposite route.

DD: Seven hours. What's that? Five hundred miles?

CH: There or thereabouts.

DD: And you passed?

CH: I did, but that was probably the most intense, and I
        guess dangerous, situation I've been in so far. Even
        worse than when we were doing the hijack work and
        the mob jumped on the car last week. At least those
        guys were acting.
              He failed my partner for the day on the route
        back just because he got us pulled over. We sped past
        a Battenberg Range Rover at a hundred miles an hour.
        I think he must have been under some illusion that
        we were invisible or the police knew what we were
        doing.

DD: What happened?

CH: The ADI flashed his police warrant card and told
        them we were in training, so it didn't go any further,
        but he missed the required time by five minutes. I
        think he's got his second and last chance to do it again
        next week.

DD: Why was it so dangerous?

CH: We were doing upwards a hundred and forty plenty
        of times. At that speed, your brain is working at such
        a rate you think you can't keep up the pace.

DD: He clearly thought you were safe and you're smiling.

CH: I loved the driving. It makes you feel alive. It was
        travelling back that was a nightmare.

DD: You weren't in control.

CH: And the instructor was actively making me distract
        the driver by pointing out each one of his fuck ups.

DD: But the other candidate didn't do this for you on the way up?

CH: No, but don't get me started on that, please.

DD: *[Laughter]* Have you missed anyone out?

[Silence]

CH: Ah, yes. Gold Instructor, Captain of Operations, aka my friend CAPOP. I'm sure he doesn't hold a grudge. *[Laughter]* Okay, I know he holds a grudge. *[Laughter]* Whenever he's the one sitting in front of me when they pull the hood off in the pamper room, as we call it, I know it's going to be a particularly uncomfortable session.

        Maybe he's like that for all of the guys, I don't know. I would ask, but you're not privy to that kind of operational information. *[Laughter]* He seems to have a fascination with the past; my past in particular. He keeps going over why my records, police, school, the Cadet Corp and Sandhurst, are so clean.

DD: Clean?

CH: Squeaky clean. No citations. No fuck ups. No bad days at the office. He thinks they're made up or I'm just too nice for this job. I tried to explain the Sandhurst graduates tend to be the conscientious type, but he didn't get it.

DD: This process does tend to attract highly driven individuals and it's rare that there haven't been any mistakes in people's pasts. A lot of the SF guys have been in trouble with the police, that kind of thing.

CH: He keeps asking me what the worst thing I've ever done is.

DD: Sounds like he's after my job, too. *[Laughter]*

CH: The last time I told him it was probably stealing a cake

110

from the cooling rack at home, but I should be forgiven because I was only five. That didn't go down well, so I offered to make something up if he preferred. He declined and I spent the next thirty minutes in the hood sitting quietly. I nearly said I could dress up as a maid if he wanted something really bad, but I kept myself in check.

DD: What about the rest? There must be another twenty instructors you come into contact with.

CH: I barely took note of them; we'll call them the averages.

DD: I don't believe that for a moment.

[Silence]

CH: *[Laughter]* Okay. You got me. There were another twenty-one in total. Sixteen male, four female, one the jury's still out. Ten were below thirty, five up to forty, the rest over the hill, but still going strong. There's another thirty-two support staff, cleaners and help in the canteen. You want their names? They were easy.

DD: *[Laughter]* No need. Thank you.

CH: Is that what you were looking for? Did you recognise any of them?

DD: That'll do fine.

[Silence]

DD: Have you seen him since we last spoke?

CH: No, but I haven't been anywhere it would be likely, unless he has clearance, of course?

DD: No need to look at me like that. I only know what you tell me.

[Silence]

111

DD: It's coming to the end of our session but I wanted to pick up on something you said before. You said you carried a knife when you tried to trap him. You never told me what you think you would have done if you'd have got hold of him?

CH: What do you think he would have done to me if he'd have gotten me?

DD: That's a question you need to answer yourself.

[Silence]

CH: Rape.

[Silence]

CH: Murder, torture first.

[Silence]

CH: Worse things my little innocent mind shouldn't even consider. I don't think it would be quick.

DD: What could be worse than rape, murder or torture?

CH: Watching as your family are raped, tortured and murdered?

[Silence]

DD: You've thought about this.

CH: Yes.

DD: So what would you have done to him?

CH: I would have made it clear that I wasn't the one for him. I would have made it impossible for him to have any interest in anyone else in the future.

[Silence]

DD: Have you ever killed anyone?

CH: What? I'm nineteen. I've never been on active service. I haven't spent even a minute with my regiment yet.

DD: Of course, but these are standard questions I need to cover.

[Silence]

DD: How would you feel if you were asked to kill someone?

CH: Would I ever kill him?

DD: No. Let's call that one a special case.

CH: On the battlefield the answer is simple. They'd be trying to kill me. Anyway, I'm a woman. We're not allowed to actively go out and kill people when we're in the forces. Yet. Self-defence only. We covered this in training too. Realities of war they called it.

DD: And it didn't faze you?

CH: It gave me a few moments of contemplation, but we already know I'd pull the trigger, don't we?

DD: Yes, but what if you were ordered to actively seek out a target and take their life? Someone who was not on the battlefield?

CH: Is that what this is? Am I applying to be an assassin?

[Silence]

CH: What had they done?

DD: You don't know. You may never find out.

CH: So why am I killing them? I take it we're not talking self-defence?

DD: No. Big picture. An order.

CH: Why am I killing them?

113

DD: You've been sent there to.

CH: By whom?

DD: Your team leader, their boss, their bosses' boss. A decision has been made.

CH: I have to trust there is a good reason?

DD: Yes.

CH: Then I would have that trust.

DD: So what if you were given the choice? What if you were told to locate the target and make an evaluation?

CH: Judge Dredd?

[Silence]

CH: I'd refer to the rules of engagement.

DD: They're open to interpretation.

CH: Then I weigh up the benefit and hope I make the right choice.

DD: What if you didn't?

CH: You tell me? Would I be in jail?

DD: It depends on how bad your choice was.

CH: No confidence in the team then?

DD: Even if you had complete immunity, you'd still have to live your life knowing what you'd done.

CH: I'd have to trust that I'd made the right call based on everything I had at hand.

DD: You have no issue with that?

CH: I hope not. I guess we'll find out if I get the job, but I would hope that I won't be put in that situation until

I've been adequately trained to make the right decision.

[Silence]

DD: Good answer. You gave back responsibility.

[Silence]

CH: Thank you.

DD: I just want to finish on a positive this session. We talk so much about the negative things that you've experienced in your life. Can you tell me about something in your past that gave you pleasure?

CH: Sure. I have plenty of happy memories, if that's what you're after. I loved my days in the Army Cadet Corp. Spending time with the platoon, climbing mountains and weekends out camping. I really got to know the leaders, and yes, the other cadets too, before you ask.

DD: But particularly the leaders?

CH: Yes. Sergeant Hopes and Willis, and Coach ████, of course. They had a great sense of humour as a team. Coach would always be winding one of the leaders up, but no one seemed to take it the wrong way. They were all there if you needed a helping hand or someone to talk to.

DD: Did you ever need someone to talk to?

CH: Not really. Not until we heard the news about Coach, of course.

[Silence]

DD: Sorry to have to leave it there, but that will have to do for today. Mealtime is ending soon and you need the calories.

[Silence]

115

DD: Oh, one thing.

CH: What's that?

DD: It's for you. *Goblet of Fire*. You said you hadn't had a chance to pick it up.

CH: Oh. Wow.

[Silence]

CH: Thank you.

DD: I have an admission. I was a little sceptical about you reading children's books when you mentioned it in our earlier session.

CH: And now you've read them?

DD: Yes. Thank you. Take it.

CH: Thank you, Dr Devlin.

Journal of Dr Devlin, Head of Occupational Psychology

Section A ███████████

1ˢᵗ November 2000 - Session 3

I'm surprised about the limited notes I've made during this session. I can still sense a reluctance to opening up. I still think she sees me as part of the process of trying to trip her up, despite my constant protests to remind her I am only observing.

However, that said, I took great insight into her need to protect her family. I was slightly chilled by her answer to what would be worse than rape, torture and murder.

When questioned about killing someone Ms H gave a robust answer, placing the responsibility with her managers to ensure she was adequately trained to make the right decision.

For the record, I gave Ms H the book to further establish our bond in order that it may break down the barrier I can still sense between us.

TRANSCRIPT OF AUDIO RECORDING A1763529-1
[DEVICE C120 COVERT RECORDER]

[DATE:1ˢᵗ DEC 2000] [09:00GMT]
[LOCATION: ████████████████████████ *]*

DD: Let's get started, shall we? What would you like to talk about today?

CH: How about we just take a moment and I have a little sleep? Say half an hour. You can write what you want. I won't mind.

DD: Very good, Miss Hughes, but I'm afraid our meetings need to be productive. How have you been?

CH: It's been a quiet few weeks.

DD: Quiet? I struggle to believe that, especially from what the other candidates are saying.

CH: Apart from the exercise we've just completed, we've been spending more time in class. The physical is still there, but it's not as relentless as it has been.

DD: What have you been learning?

CH: Field craft mainly, but lots of weapons training, too.

DD: You're smiling. Don't tell me you're enjoying the process?

CH: The classroom stuff is great. Learning lots of new skills and, of course, playing with guns is always enjoyable.

DD: So you're not enjoying every aspect?

CH: We've been separated out into squads of six and kept apart from the other candidates, including whilst in the classroom. We're sleeping in the same room, messing and training together.

DD: Are you feeling claustrophobic?

CH: It's not that. It's just there's a general feeling that something is about to kick off and this group wouldn't be my number one pick.

DD: You think you're going out in the field again? What's the exercise?

CH: We haven't been told but we're all pretty sure something's coming up.

[Silence]

DD: Who is in your squad?

CH: *[Deep sigh]* Thirty-seven. An uber fit Flathead, sorry Desmond. He's taken the time to grow a long beard since he'd been on my minibus for Evasion One and for some reason he'd decided to shave his hair. I thought it might all be getting to him, but Nick still won't shut up with the constant banter. He looks more like a biker than elite special forces, but that's their thing.

DD: First name terms now?

CH: It's a necessity. We're working all day long together as a team so we had to choose something rather than using our numbers. Seems like the instructors don't care as long as we don't use real names.

DD: Do I have to guess?

CH: It's pretty benign, I'm afraid. He likes golf, so Nick Faldo it is.

DD: I take it he's not one of those you were referring to with your previous comment?

CH: I guess not. He's pretty handy to have around.

DD: And the others?

CH: The three weakest links.

[Silence]

CH: What?

DD: That's a pretty arrogant statement. They're quite someway down the line in the process now.

CH: It's a scale, even if it's still at the top of the measure. I guess it takes a certain level of arrogance to get to this stage, too, don't you think?

[Silence]

CH: Both Nick and I are of the same opinion. I'm trying not to take it personally that the instructors have lumped us with the three frailest candidates still left in the process.

DD: Is that fair? Have you considered that they may have put all the weakest candidates together?

[Silence]

CH: I'll let you have that one and it's not about being fair. Surely the whole point of this process is to weed out those who are not going to be suitable? Those who are too weak?

DD: I'm sure you understand that strength can be measured in different ways.

[Silence]

DD: Why don't you tell me about them.

[Silence]

CH: We have a spook. Domestic. No tan. He was the one that gave me the black eye; a training accident if I'm in a good mood, incompetence if I'm not. Or he could be working with the instructors to pull me down. A mole, perhaps.

DD: Do you really think that?

CH: This whole process makes you paranoid.

[Silence]

[Laughter]

DD: What's funny?

CH: He always seems to eye me with suspicion as if I was out to get him, but it just occurred to me. I wonder if he thinks the same about me.

DD: Were you out to get him?

CH: Not particularly. Of course, I never held back when we were paired in hand to hand.

DD: Did he get a name?

CH: Nigel.

DD: What's behind the name?

CH: Nothing.

DD: Oh.

[Silence]

DD: Carry on.

CH: There was another spook, light-skinned too. Homer, a GCHQ geek.

DD: I get it, doughnuts. I really don't understand on what you're basing these guesses.

CH: I'm just very observant. Then it's a process of elimination. Of course, I could well be wrong, but I can't ask them outright. We're not supposed to know anything about each other's real lives. I bet you know though.

DD: Good try. So what makes you believe Mr Homer works for GCHQ?

CH: Homer. Just Homer. Have you ever seen an episode of the Simpsons?

[Silence]

CH: Never mind. He's always talking about the tech. He loves the classroom stuff but you can see him pull back at unannounced PT. I really don't think he knew what he was getting into here.

        He has the hair of a teenager, short at the sides, long and curled at the top. A proper ginge; like really deep red and a weird looking goatee too. Big headphones always straddling his head at every free moment. Always asks me questions and has a nervous presence. He's really self-conscious of getting something wrong. Apart from that, he's fine.

DD: I'm sure they have their useful sides for the operational environment too? The instructors must be able to see something you don't.

CH: Want someone followed? Send the spook. Got a bit of broken kit or need IT support? Homer's your man. Need to live in the mud evading a hostile force for two weeks? 'Fraid not.

DD: How do you know all this?

CH: Five days on Salisbury Plain is very revealing, but that's a story for another time, I think.

[Silence]

CH: And they're not even the worst. I haven't mentioned Edith, a detective with the MET, if the accent was anything to go by.

DD: So you're not swapping stories? How do you have any idea she's a detective?

CH: I met quite a few detectives when the police were investigating the kidnapping. They have a common air, a drive and maybe just a way they look out on life. They deal with the dregs of humanity and I think that shows through. Edith has the same look.

        Like I said, I might be wrong, but hey, it passes the time.

DD: Go on, tell me so we can move on.

CH: Edith Smith, the first female police officer with arrest powers and everything. She's not so keen on the name, but she got the reference and must have thought it was better than sixty-one.

        When we were on exercise, she also wasn't so keen on the mud, more than the other two, which is saying something. *[Laughter]* Although seeing their grimaces as we laid up was a high point of that day.

DD: Is there a chance you're being particularly hard on the other female in the squad?

CH: What, because I wanted to be the centre of attention, or maybe she's letting the sisterhood down?

DD: Is it?

CH: No. It's because she's a liability, likely to get me and the other three kicked off the course.

DD: You don't get to be a detective in the MET by being a delicate flower. She's been on the course for the same amount of time as you. Are you sure you're not being too hard on her?

[Silence]

DD: You don't have to answer, but I get the impression you don't want to get on with anyone and you're

123

finding faults to give yourself a reason.

CH: Shall we swap places and see what you think?

[Silence]

CH: You're right I'm not getting on with anyone and that's deliberate. I do enough to stay in the loop, like we discussed before. I keep aloof. Most of these people will be out of my life for good in a few months' time.

DD: One way or another. How were they towards you?

CH: Fine.

DD: Very descriptive.

[Silence]

DD: Where's Stacey all this time?

CH: She's not in my squad. I think they left us apart deliberately. Have you been talking to them about us?

[Silence]

CH: Okay. From the time we were put in squads we haven't seen much of anyone else. We're just too busy, in different areas of the camp and sleep is a priority when we're not busting ourselves open.

DD: So you haven't spoken to her in five weeks?

[Silence]

CH: No.

[Silence]

CH: I mean yes.

[Silence]

CH: We meet up a few times on the sly for a chat and a download.

DD: A few times?

CH: Every so often.

DD: I get the distinct feeling you're not telling me everything.

CH: Okay. We meet most nights.

DD: How do you manage that?

CH: I'm sorry, but I'm not willing to reveal that kind of operational information. *[Laughter]*

DD: *[Laughter]* Okay, I get it. *[Laughter]* This must be strange for you. Being so close to someone who isn't your family, I mean?

CH: Hey, look, I don't mind admitting, but I think we're closer than family. She's kind of my first proper friend.

DD: That's nice. I sense you're worried about her?

CH: A bit. I don't know how she'll cope. I sometimes come close to the edge myself.

DD: And you think you're stronger than her? Again, she hasn't got this far without being able to handle herself. Unless you're saying that your help is what's getting her this far?

CH: That's not what I'm saying. We're all close to the edge, but the only person I'm in control of is me.

[Silence]

CH: She *can* handle herself.

DD: And if she can't?

CH: She'll be sent back to her regiment.

DD: Does that bother you?

125

[Silence]

CH: I don't know. If I fail as well then fine, we can carry on being friends. I don't know what it'll mean if I get through and she doesn't.

DD: Or the other way around.

[Knock at the door]

DD: Come in.

[Unidentified Voice]

UV: Sorry, sir, we need the candidate.

DD: Okay. Corra, good luck.

CH: Thank you.

Journal of Dr Devlin, Head of Occupational Psychology

Section A ▓▓▓▓▓▓▓▓▓▓▓▓

1st December 2000 - Session 4

Ms H has a real love of weapons that comes across in her manner and demeanour when she talks about weapons training and spending her time on the range. From all accounts, this also comes through in her achievements and scores in all the related assessments. I believe this to be harmless enough, despite how some of my colleagues think it is unhealthy. It has been a constant in her life since the time when she joined the Cadet Corp and her life took a new direction. There is a possibility that the weapons serve as some sort of security blanket against her demons.

Ms H displays a high level of arrogance when she talks about some of her colleagues in the process. At least now they have been given names, which should help to personalise them for her.

When I confronted her about her arrogance, she didn't believe this to be a negative. She is right to a certain degree, but as with everything, there is a thin line whereby this trait could affect her decision-making process. She does, however, lack the maturity to understand that strength is not about who can carry the most weight or be ahead on the march, shoot the bullseye or even solve the puzzle the quickest. This, I believe, is due to the significant age gap between the other candidates.

Again, she shows a tendency to paranoia about being specifically targeted in the process by the instructors. I know this could well be the case; the team have been known to push the stronger ones harder than the others to see what it brings out. She did, however, seem to have a breakthrough about this during our conversation. I look forward to seeing how this affects her attitude towards the rest of the candidates.

Ms H referred to a recent exercise on Salisbury plain in our conversation. I understand from the instructors that she aced the challenge, not only capturing the flag on her own, but she brought it back to her team rather than keeping for herself. Only one other member of her team made it back, but I'm told they were not able to cope with the rather extreme method Ms H, as squad leader, chose for evading the force trying to hunt her down. This is some progress on team dynamics, despite her words to the contrary.

We touched on a possible reasoning for her forced isolation. She seems to be opening up a little, even if it is just a crack.

When I turned the conversation to Stacey, I was surprised to see Ms H getting flustered, offering a physical reaction to the subject. Her cheeks were reddening and she wouldn't look me in the eye for a few moments. Until now, our eye contact has been nearly unmoving. In the end, she used comedy for light relief.

TRANSCRIPT OF AUDIO RECORDING A1763529-1
[DEVICE C120 COVERT RECORDER]

[DATE:8th DEC 2000] [10:11GMT]
[LOCATION: ▮▮▮▮▮▮▮▮▮▮▮▮▮▮▮▮▮▮▮▮▮ *]*

CH: Is he okay?

DD: I don't know what you're talking about.

CH: Twenty-one. Is he dead?

[Silence]

CH: He's dead, isn't he? He looked awful. Have you heard?

DD: I haven't heard anything.

CH: That's good, isn't it?

DD: I wouldn't draw any inference from it. I'm outside of the operational loop as I've said before. What's happened? Take a deep breath.

CH: It was… it was… must be three days or so ago now, part way through exercise. I've literally just arrived and they bundled me into the shower and clean clothes and now into here. They won't tell me anything. Are you going to tell me he's dead?

DD: This is your scheduled session. I have no idea about what has happened. Take a deep breath and stay there. I'll see what I can find out.

CH: Thank you.

[Silence]

[Deep, slow breaths in the background]

DD: Here, eat these. You sound like you need some sugar.
        [Ruffling of plastic]

[Silence]

129

DD: You should be eating those.

CH: *[Barely discernible]* Is he okay?

DD: I still don't know. I've sent a message out. Take some time, eat and tell me what's been happening.

[Silence]

DD: Tell me from the beginning.

[Silence]

CH: Okay. When I left the last session, I had time to change into jeans and grab a coat then go straight to a waiting minibus and the rest of the squad. Archie was in the driver's seat, briefing us as we joined the motorway. Maybe the word briefing is overdoing it just a little.

       We'd been right about the exercise. He started listing five addresses in London to each of our blank faces. Then he said at each address we would have to obtain a flag. We weren't allowed to use any of our contacts from our previous lives and were not allowed to cause damage to the target addresses. This rule intrigued me the most.

       At a sixth address in the suburbs of London, we would rendezvous with a chopper in a week's time.

DD: So you had a week to get five flags and then get a helicopter ride home. There must have been a catch.

CH: Of course there was a catch. We all knew he wasn't telling us everything and he was loving every second of watching our mixture of excitement and intrigue.

       As we pulled off the motorway at Slough and stopped at the side of the slip-road, he told us to piss off. Homer was the last to get off and just as he did, Archie told him to grab the small ruck in the passenger footwell.

130

DD: Is that twenty-one?

CH: Yes. As soon as Homer grabbed the bag and jumped to the Tarmac, Archie shouted out of the door that there was another team being dropped off at the same time, at an equal distance to where we were and they had the same targets.

        The team with the most flags would be the only group getting a lift home. Laughing his head off, he drove away, leaving us in no doubt that if we failed to get on the chopper, not only would we have to make our own way back to the training camp, we were probably going to get booted off the course, or at least some of us would.

DD: But this is the kind of thing you love.

CH: Yes. Despite the freezing cold.

DD: What was in the bag?

CH: It was pretty much empty apart from a small document wallet containing about a thousand pounds in twenties. I had to check a second time to make sure they really hadn't given us a copy of the addresses he'd reeled off.

DD: Did anyone remember them? Don't tell me, Homer has an eidetic memory?

CH: No and No. I remember the sinking feeling when I tried to recall the addresses. I reckon I could maybe get the rendezvous point, but the rest were no good. Equally, each of the others had the same expression, apart from Edith. She pulled out a small notebook and showed us the scribbled addresses.

DD: She's not all bad then.

CH: And clearly a copper.

DD: So you were on the outskirts of London and had to

find five addresses. You had a MET detective with you. That sounds a little too easy for my liking.

CH: Yeah, about that. I thought the same too, but knowing the instructors know a lot more, if not everything about us, I wasn't doing a victory dance.

[Silence]

CH: Is something funny?

DD: Sorry. No. I just can't get the image of you doing a victory dance out of my mind.

CH: I'll carry on while that passes, shall I?

DD: Yes. Please do.

CH: Despite our concerns, we weren't going to waste the possible advantage we'd been given. Perhaps the others were given a spy who used to be a black cab driver. We didn't know.

Turns out she knew the addresses were all garbage. The road names were fine; she had a passing familiarity with each of the areas, but the building numbers were just way too long. They were six or more numbers. I've never seen a building number that looks like an American zip code before.

DD: Why didn't you just ask her there and then if she was a police officer? Who would know?

CH: As much as I don't mind bending the rules a little, I'd had it made clear that I needed to follow the rules and I didn't want to risk it. Apparently, no one else did either.

DD: And you wouldn't tell me anyway because you still think I'm linked to the operational process.

[Silence]

132

CH: We followed signs towards the town centre and agreed the priorities were to identify the target addresses or decipher whatever the code was and make our way to the area. The five addresses were all over London.

DD: I'm intrigued how, using your assessment, two spies, a detective, a special forces operator, an engineer and an officer in the military got into London?

CH: Is that how you see me?

[Silence]

DD: Sorry, what do you mean?

CH: Well, do you see me as a military officer?

DD: You seem disappointed?

CH: No. No. Just curious. Anyway, it doesn't matter.

DD: Okay. How do you see yourself?

CH: It doesn't matter, like I said. In answer to your question, we got the train. Remember we had the cash.
        We got a phone book in Paddington and booked up a cheap hotel; it was getting dark by the time we arrived. Trying to conserve the money, we took two rooms and crammed everyone in. We thought we should have enough cash for the week but I suggested everyone have a think about how we could raise more money if we needed to. But we couldn't steal or rob anyone.

DD: Did you feel you needed to make that point to the group?

CH: It was the obvious way to get hold of cash quickly, but the group agreed with me without any complaint. We pretty quickly split into two groups, Edith, myself

133

and Homer. The other team were to familiarise themselves with the local area and form a security plan.

DD: A security plan?

CH: Identify escape routes, points of possible surveillance, CCTV, diversions we could use if the place became compromised.

DD: Compromised by who?

CH: The other team. Or the instructors, police. There's a long list.

DD: So what was your task and how did you feel about being put with those two?

CH: It was my decision.

DD: Not a group decision?

CH: No. After a brief discussion, we agreed it would be best if I was squad leader.

DD: How did that make you feel that they wanted you as squad leader?

CH: I was a little surprised. Maybe they thought I was a little opinionated and it would be one way of keeping me sweet.

DD: Or maybe your aloofness didn't work and they saw that you had the skills they might need to lead them into completing the task. Perhaps they didn't have such a low opinion of you as you do of them.

CH: I don't have a low opinion of them.

[Silence]

CH: Raise your eyebrows all you want.

[Silence]

134

CH: Okay, maybe I had been a little harsh before I got to find out what they were really like.

DD: Maybe it should have been something you did before you deployed.

CH: I guess so. Maybe things would have turned out a little different.

DD: I wasn't suggesting that you were the cause of whatever has happened to Homer. I still don't know what happened. Please, carry on.

[Silence]

CH: Homer wanted us to see if we could use one of the hotel's computers, but the owners weren't having any of it. Going the extra mile for their customers wasn't one of their strong selling points. Instead, I found a newsagent, grabbed an A-Z map book and took it back to the hotel.

        The other three had left the hotel at this point so we poured over it in what was now our sub-squad bedroom. The streets were easy to find but it was Homer who spotted the one common feature on each of them. A bank. An independent bank, not one of your high street Barclays or Abbey National. A quick call to directory enquiries and we had their addresses. I'd barely written the first one down before Homer cracked the problem with the addresses.

        The last two digits of the number were the building number and the rest were safety deposit box numbers. We didn't need to ring any more; he'd figured it out.

DD: So?

CH: Yes, they were proving me wrong. I'm happy to admit it. Go on, write it down.

DD: I will. *[Laughter]* In bold.

[Silence]

DD: It must have been getting late by now?

CH: Early evening. Too late to do much more with the banks other than try to figure out how we were going to get into five safety deposit boxes without breaking them open.

DD: Three boxes. You only needed to get into three. You just had to stop the other team getting more than you.

CH: It crossed my mind, but not for long. I wanted to do this properly. I certainly didn't want to scrape by.

DD: Is that what the others wanted?

CH: I was squad leader by then so I didn't ask for feedback. I also thought about just getting one then making it impossible for the other team to get into the other four, but all my ideas involved things getting broken.

DD: So you all had an early night to be ready for the action in the morning?

CH: I couldn't help thinking that if we cracked the code so easily then the other team would be in the same position.

DD: So you went out to scope the banks.

CH: Yes.

DD: And you went alone.

CH: How did you know?

DD: You told the other two to get some rest so they would be fresh for the morning.

CH: I think we're spending too much time together.

DD: *[Laughter]* Please continue.

CH: Do you think they would have heard back yet? Can
       you check?

DD: Okay. Give me a minute.

Journal of Dr Devlin, Head of Occupational Psychology

Section A ████████████████

8th December 2000 - Session 5.1

Ms H showed what appears to be real emotion over the incident with candidate twenty-one. I was surprised to hear that she was so willing to talk to me despite her agitation and need to get answers.

For the second time, when I referred to Ms H as a military officer, she seemed to take exception. She wouldn't elaborate when asked and I'm curious to find out why. Perhaps she already sees herself in the new position. However, I don't know how much she knows about the role.

If the group did indeed make Ms H squad leader, which I have no reason to doubt, this is another example of how reality seems to go against her perceptions of herself, or at least her preference of being alone. It would be useful at this stage to get the opinions of those within the group. However, this would be without precedent in this process. This could be a breakthrough in not only realising she needs to be an effective member of a team but also that teamwork has major benefits for her and her goals. Is she learning that it is okay to work *with* others?

TRANSCRIPT OF AUDIO RECORDING A1763529-1
[DEVICE C120 COVERT RECORDER]

[DATE:8th DEC 2000] [11:21GMT]
[LOCATION: ███████████████████████ *]*

CH: Any news?

DD: No. Afraid not. Are you okay to continue?

CH: Yes. Yes. I'd rather be doing something. You were a long time; I thought there might have been news.

DD: No. I had to wait and took the time to write up my notes. Where did you go from the hotel whilst Homer and Edith were resting?

CH: I left them setting up a card game and ended up visiting the closest three sites, getting the last tube back to the hotel. I didn't see any activity of interest but at least I had a picture in my head of what we were up against, from the outside at least.

        The next day I planned for us to visit each of the locations and enquire about getting safety deposit boxes. I also had a plan to stakeout each of the locations so we could track down the other team and keep up to date with their progress.

DD: How did that go?

CH: Pretty well. All but Homer were suited to the task, bread and butter. We had to take a risk on Homer being able to watch one of the locations whilst I went to the banks and made the enquiries.

DD: How did you communicate with each other if you were spread out across London?

CH: I didn't want to use up a load of the money buying mobile phones, so I bought one for myself and had the rest of the team check in regularly via phone boxes.

DD: And what did you find out?

CH: I managed to visit each one, confirming each of the deposit box numbers existed in each of the banks and proving Homer had been right about the codes. No one reported any signs of the other team by the time the places closed.

DD: Did you have a plan of how to get into the boxes?

CH: No. Not at this stage, but I was forming a backup plan. I wouldn't say I was panicking but I was getting nervous that we'd had two days already but with no flags to show for it.

DD: What was the backup plan?

CH: Track down the other team, let them do all the hard work of getting the flags then steal them from under their noses.

DD: That doesn't sound like you?

CH: I know. That's why it was the backup plan. I didn't sleep much that night. Breaking into the banks wasn't going to be possible. It would take so much time to organise and we just didn't have the capability. It would be difficult not to break the rule about damage.
        The only way we could safely get the boxes open would be to either get the customer key, or somehow convince the bank that one of us was the legitimate customer for the box and we'd lost the key so they would break it open, no doubt charging a small fortune in the process if we managed to do the impossible.

DD: It's a tricky one. Why are you looking at me like that?

CH: I'm just intrigued. How many people have sat in front of you explaining this problem to you? You must have heard so many different ways of completing this exercise?

DD: Based on our previous conversations, I doubt you will believe me when I say this exercise is different every year.

CH: Humph. Okay, you could have just said you're not able to tell me.

DD: I did say you wouldn't believe me. Anyway, how did *you* solve the problem?

CH: It was Homer really.

[Silence]

CH: I knew you'd smile. I'll just say it now, okay? I was wrong to judge these people before I got to know them.

[Silence]

CH: Homer came up with the idea of hacking into the bank's computers. All he needed was a computer and a floppy disk and he could write a simple keyboard logger. It would record every single keystroke the user enters, including their passwords for the customer records or database. From there we could work to obtain the keys.

DD: Sounds simple enough. *[Laughter]*

CH: The computer was easy. That night whilst the management were asleep, I think there was just one duty staff member on site. We broke into the staff area of the hotel and Homer worked through the night to create the programme we needed. He was so happy when he saw the computer was still running Windows 95.

DD: Why was that?

CH: I'm guessing it was just easier and yes, before you ask, I was impressed. Nick and I took it in turns to keep watch whilst the others slept, but by the early morning we had all we needed for the first part. Unfortunately, we needed Homer for the second half of the solution as he was the only one who could install the software.

DD: Why unfortunately?

CH: He'd been working all through the night. At least Nick and I had been able to rest when we weren't on look out. Plus, we cope with the lack of sleep better.

DD: Was he struggling?

CH: A little. His response times were slower and he was a little dazed, but nothing too bad at that stage. The great part about what he wrote is he didn't need to know the bank computer's password to install the software. All he had to do was put in the disk, turn the computer off and on again at the wall and the software would do the rest. There were a few commands to type after that which he said depended on the operating system, so he had to come along.

[Silence]

CH: Yes, I was even more impressed.
        The next challenge was getting to the computers. This also wasn't a big issue, but it did mean we had to sacrifice our surveillance on the banks. I needed all but one of the team to carry out my plan.

DD: I'm intrigued.

CH: It's not elegant, I'm afraid.

DD: Go ahead.

CH: I'd already been to each of the banks, so I could only pose as a customer, which I did, and with a quick shopping trip we had Homer dressed like a plumber. Whilst I was in the bank asking more questions, along with Edith and Nick also posing as separate customers, Homer turned the water off in the street and announced himself as being from the water board calling about the loss of water.

He was there to test the taps and toilet. These were only small banks so with most of the staff occupied with either helping us, other customers and the rest going around the building flushing toilets and running taps, Homer installed his programme in seconds.

DD: That sounds elegant to me.

CH: Well, as I say it back, it does sound better.

DD: And you were able to do this at each of the banks?

CH: No. At the third one, Homer couldn't find where to turn the water off in the street. He still tried the ruse but when they said they still had water he didn't push it any further.

DD: And how did you take that?

CH: What do you mean?

DD: I expected you weren't too happy with his performance?

CH: On the contrary. I knew he was already way out of his comfort zone and applauded him for not pushing further and risking the staff calling the police.

DD: Oh. That's great.

CH: Maybe you've got me wrong, Doctor.

DD: Or maybe you're learning.

[Silence]

DD: You got four sets of passwords?

CH: No. We ran out of time on the fifth.

DD: You had to settle for going after three flags?

CH: I should have.

DD: Are you okay? Do you want some water?

CH: No. I'm fine.

DD: Okay. How did you get hold of the passwords? I assume you had to go back to the banks to get the passwords and access the computers?

CH: That's what I thought, but no. Homer's programme sent the results of the keylogger across the internet. He told me all the glorious details, but they're gone now.

DD: Are you sure you don't want a break?

[Silence]

CH: We repeated the use of the hotel's computer in the dead of night and he managed to access their databases remotely. It's scary what you can do if you know how. We had three names and addresses of key holders.

DD: And this is on day…?

CH: Day four. Three days left to get the next two sets of details, track down the other team and burgle three houses. With about three hours sleep for me and Homer, we were out again the next day on surveillance. I had Steve on the first of the houses, Nick on the other, then I split the rest of us between the four banks, watching for the other team.

144

DD: Steve?

CH: MI6.

[Silence]

DD: How did you decide which one not to keep an eye on?

CH: The closest to us and one which we had successfully hacked access to the box's owner. I figured we had more to lose on the two we didn't have the details for.
       I'd been in place at the third bank for about an hour, one of the two we hadn't got into, when I got a call from Steve. He said there was an opportunity to get into the house. There were no cars outside and no sign of anyone at home. Not having any reports from the others, I told him to wait. I headed to Homer's location and told him to head to bank three whilst I checked out the house with Steve.
       Looking back, he looked dog-tired.

DD: Like you.

CH: Yes, but I was fine. Tired, but still operating well.

DD: Was he making mistakes?

CH: No, but with hindsight the signs were getting worse.

[Silence]

DD: What did you find at the target house? I'm assuming from your expression it didn't go well.

CH: Actually, the opposite. Heading to meet up with Steve, I got a call from Nigel.

[Silence]

CH: MI5.

DD: Ah yes.

CH: He'd spotted two members of the other team and followed them on the tube. He was making the call from outside a hotel they'd headed into. I made a judgement call and diverted to the hotel and Nigel. I knew when I failed to meet Steve at the agreed time, he'd call and I could fill him in.

        Everything was going really well. By the time I got to the hotel, Steve called to say he went ahead with the burglary and he had the key. We practically had the first flag. I re-tasked him to take Nick and do the same with the second address.

DD: But your expression doesn't match the positive progress you were making.

CH: I'm getting there.

DD: Sorry. Please continue.

CH: It was about midday by now and I was talking over the options with Nigel about how to play it, whether to tie up our team to keep them under surveillance or to just watch the hotel.

        We were going over what we knew about the pair from the other team; a couple of spooks or special forces, the line was blurred on these two. We hadn't come to any conclusion on what to do next when we saw four people leave the hotel. In the lead were the two Nigel had tracked, then another guy, but walking at his side was Stacey.

[Silence]

DD: It was bound to happen.

CH: What was?

DD: Eventually you would be on different sides of the table and only one of you was going to win. As the process goes on, the likelihood was getting larger.

CH: I knew all this.

DD: I'm sure you did. How did it make you feel?

CH: I recognised it but made no alterations to my plans.

DD: I don't get that impression from the way you were talking earlier.

CH: Are you suggesting that I was anything but professional, and that I changed my approach because of who was on the other team? I still had an objective to complete.

DD: No. I'm not suggesting that. All I'm suggesting is you may have taken a moment to think about how you felt about the situation.

CH: I was fine. By this time, the information from the teams was coming in thick and fast. The second house the team went to had a police car outside; we'd have to assume we were already too late and the other team clearly didn't do a discrete job. I despatched the team to check out the last key holder's address and to pick up the flag so we at least had one in the bag.

       We decided it was time to push our luck a little and stayed with their hotel rather than trying to follow them.

DD: Yours or a group decision?

CH: Ultimately mine, but none of those I was in touch with put up any complaint. It would be too much of a risk to follow these guys for a prolonged time, and labour intensive. As soon as we knew there was none of the team in the rooms, we'd turn it over.

DD: What did you expect to find?

CH: Not sure. Names and addresses, safety deposit box keys maybe.

[Silence]

CH: We rented a room in their hotel, which gave us a reason to be inside and luckily, like our hotel, they'd decided to go down the cheap route. I stayed at the room with Steve, leaving Nigel to go back to our hotel as he had already been around them too long and was at risk of being spotted.

        We soon found their rooms; again they were sharing two, but they weren't next to each other, which made life a lot easier.

DD: How did they get on with the third address?

CH: It was some gated mansion in Belgravia with CCTV and three parked cars on the gravel drive. Nightmare place to hit. It would take a lot of time.

DD: You gave up on it?

CH: No, but we put it to one side whilst we evaluated our options.

[Silence]

CH: Morning came and I briefed everyone one by one as they called in from their positions. Firstly, speaking with Homer, telling them all about the success of the previous day, whilst making it clear we were probably on the back foot.

        We knew they had at least the same number of keys as us (assuming they'd hit the place with the police car) and the next three keys were going to be a challenge; if we could get one of them it could make or break the whole exercise.

        I cut the last briefing short when Steve spotted the other team leaving in two groups. Moments later, I got a call from Homer.

        He was at the fifth bank and kept trying to explain the situation, saying over and over the timing was right, asking me if he could go in. I said I would join him but first I had to break into the hotel room, telling him I was twenty minutes away, if that, and I'd be on my way as soon as possible.

[Silence]

CH: I told him to wait where he was. I told him not to do anything until I got there.

DD: How long did it take you to meet with him?

CH: About an hour and a half.

DD: What took you so long? Were there problems with getting into the room?

CH: Not really. I managed to get the keys for the room. The security of the hotel, like ours, was shocking. A simple distraction and Steve had the spare key within a few seconds.

DD: Did you find anything of use?

CH: A flag.

DD: Oh, wow. You found a flag. They couldn't have hidden it very well.

CH: It was in the safe.

[Silence]

DD: How did you get into the safe?

CH: I'd dusted the keypad with the milk powder you get in the complimentary tea and coffee. The biggest pain was clearing it up afterwards.

DD: You'll have to explain.

CH: The milk powder sticks to the grease from your fingertips, like a low-tech version of fingerprint powder. The more powder that sticks, the greater the highlight of the more recently used keys. It gave me the four digits I needed. I just didn't know the order they were used in.

DD: Is this something we've taught you?

CH: No.

DD: So where…?

CH: I pick things up and it's pretty logical if you think about it.

DD: I never would have thought to do that.

CH: I should hope not. It's not your line of work.

DD: Or yours yet. How did you figure out the order?

CH: Got lucky, I guess. Why are you frowning?

DD: Lucky. Is anyone that lucky?

CH: Okay. I realised the digits were the day, month and year of Stacey's birthday.

DD: You know her birthday? I thought you were forbidden from telling each other personal details.

[Silence]

CH: She never told me.

[Silence]

DD: Should I ask?

[Silence]

DD: Never mind. It sounds like that part should have been quick. What took you so long to get to Homer? Assuming you did.

CH: I did. I bumped into Stacey on the way out.

DD: She caught you?

CH: I was out of the hotel. In fact, nearly at the tube station. I was heading in and she was heading out. I quite literally nearly bumped into her.

DD: Was she as surprised to see you?

CH: She was.

DD: Did you go back to the hotel?

CH: No. Of course not.

[Silence]

CH: Why would we go back to the hotel?

DD: Never mind. Did you explain why you were there?

CH: I didn't mention it. We went for coffee and talked. It was nice to be out in the open and not in the confines of this place.

DD: What did you talk about? Did she guess that you'd found the hotel? Sorry for the multiple questions.

CH: We didn't talk about the operation, if that's what you mean. She was surprised to see me though, yes.

DD: So what did you tell her?

CH: I told her I was looking for her.

DD: That's bold.

CH: It was the first thing that came into my mind. And it wasn't a lie, it was just a little delayed.

DD: Did she suspect anything?

CH: Of course she did. She wanted to know how I knew she was on the operation. She wanted to know how I found her. All I told her was that one of our team

151

followed one of her team but lost her here and I was staking the place out. She wasn't naive enough to ask much more. I guess she knew she wouldn't get a straight answer.

DD: Then what happened?

CH: We caught up. It was like we took a pause on the process. We didn't talk about the operation beyond what I said. We drank our coffees and then I said I would be on my way. We made no pacts or arrangements. She watched me head off to the tube station. I don't doubt she made sure I'd gone and we went our separate ways.

DD: How did meeting her make you feel?

[Silence]

CH: It was nice.

DD: Nice?

CH: Nice to see her.

DD: How did it feel that you were on the other side of the coin and you'd broken into her hotel room and used her personal information to get the flag?

CH: Yes, I felt bad. Is that what you want to hear?

DD: If it's the truth.

CH: What else could I do? I wasn't going to choose a friendship over a career.

DD: How do you think she felt? She must know it was you who took the flag from the hotel room?

CH: I hope she would understand. Can we move on please? I thought you wanted to know about…

DD: Homer. Yes, please.

CH: Before I even left the tube station at the fifth bank, I heard the sirens, despite the heavy rain which seemed to come from nowhere. It was bright sunshine as I entered the tube station only twenty minutes before.

The sirens weren't an unusual sound for London but I feared the worst. I looked over to the café we'd been using for the surveillance and he wasn't there. The door of the bank burst open and there was Homer with his face wide with panic. No one followed him but a police car raced around the corner, dodging the thin traffic and heading right for him.

I called out and he looked straight at me, his face lit up like I was his saviour and he changed direction, running into the road. He hadn't seen the police car.

[Silence]

CH: It hit him.

DD: Do you need a moment?

CH: No. It's fine.

[Silence]

CH: I watched him fly through the air. The police car tried to stop but the road was too wet and they were travelling too fast. Before they'd even got out of the car another police car rounded the corner. Two cops jumped out of the second car with MP5s waving around at everyone trying to figure out what had happened, but within seconds they'd surrounded Homer giving first aid.

DD: What did you do?

CH: I froze. I watched. I didn't know what to do.

[Silence]

CH: Should I have helped?

DD: Could you have been any help?

[Silence]

CH: I didn't do anything for a long time. It felt like a long
        time anyway. When the ambulance arrived, I left.

DD: How did he look?

CH: He hadn't moved since he'd landed on the ground.

[Silence]

CH: If I hadn't have waited and talked with Stacey…

[Silence]

DD: You told him not to go in.

CH: But I didn't tell him we had two flags and I stressed
        to him, to everyone, how key the next flag would be.
        He must have felt under a lot of pressure. Too much
        maybe.

[Silence]

DD: What happened after you left?

CH: I regretted leaving and tried to figure out which
        hospital they took him to.

DD: What was the alternative?

CH: I could have stayed with him.

DD: You'd have been implicated in whatever the police
        were racing to the scene for.

CH: Does that matter now?

DD: You tell me. I'm not judging you. I just want to hear
        what you think.

[Silence]

CH: I think I contributed to his…

[Silence]

CH: …accident. I think I should have read him better and shouldn't have spent that time with Stacey.

DD: Why do you think you misread him?

CH: I got distracted.

DD: Do you think you could read him? From what you said about him, about each of your teammates prior to the exercise, you would have had to get to know them a lot better.

CH: And I did.

[Silence]

DD: Has your opinion changed?

CH: Yes.

DD: In what way?

[Silence]

CH: I couldn't help but get to know them. Each of them deserves to be in the process. Even Homer. What he did with the hacking into the computers, with so many other things. He's a genius.

[Silence]

DD: Do you want to take a break?

CH: Only so you can check to see if there's any news.

Journal of Dr Devlin, Head of Occupational Psychology

Section A ▉▉▉▉▉▉▉

8th December 2000 - Session 5.2

Ms H appears to have had a breakthrough and she freely admitted it. It would seem that she acted like a good team leader and not just an authoritative hot head as I would have expected.

Despite her protests earlier and somewhat today as well, Ms H has been talking on a personal level with at least one candidate. Stacey. It is difficult to identify if the relationship is anything but friendship. The pointers are certainly there but it could be that Ms H is just excited for what she called her first real friend. It was particularly interesting that she spent more time with Stacey than she needed when they bumped into each other. Ms H clearly feels this was a mistake and it was her personal life getting in the way of her career. I think she may have learnt a valuable and painful lesson.

Despite all of this, when she said she wouldn't choose a friend over her career, I believed her. I think she is so focused on this role, on any role, that she would give up her relationships.

TRANSCRIPT OF AUDIO RECORDING A1763529-1
[DEVICE C120 COVERT RECORDER]

[DATE:8th DEC 2000] [12:09GMT]
[LOCATION: ███████████████████ *]*

CH: Anything?

DD: I'm afraid not.

[Silence]

DD: Shall we carry on?

[Silence]

DD: What happened after the accident?

CH: I pulled everyone back to regroup, meeting at a bar just in case our hotel had been compromised. I told them about Homer and laid it on the line. I gave them the decision to carry on or to check out if he was okay.

DD: You deferred to the group?

CH: Yes. It felt pretty alien, but it wasn't just my career I would be putting on the line if I concentrated on Homer.

DD: We may be making progress. And the group decided...?

CH: To carry on with the mission. With two flags now in hand and two flags reasonably up for grabs, we agreed that protecting our flags had to be a top priority. Once the other group found out what we'd done then their best chance would be to hit us rather than chase the two remaining flags, which were the hardest of the targets.

     We agreed to change hotels and Nick would take control of the flags, not making contact with us again until the rendezvous point, whilst we would concentrate on the other three flags.

DD: Which were?

CH: Banks three and five, plus the Belgravia house, of course. We couldn't decide which would be the easier.

DD: With four of you left, how did you get the rest of the flags.

CH: We didn't. I thought it was too risky. Instead, I decided we'd track the other team, starting at the two remaining banks. If we saw them succeed then we'd hit them. They were the weakest link.

DD: Let them do the hard work, then steal from them again?

CH: Yes, but more significantly, let them take the risk of getting caught. Without Homer…

[Silence]

CH: …we were down to brute force and we weren't allowed to break anything in the bank.

DD: How did you feel when the deadline came and you only had two flags?

CH: Okay. We were reasonably sure the other team hadn't been able to secure the flags. There had been no activity around the two banks and they certainly hadn't caught up with us. We just had to hope they hadn't intercepted Nick.

DD: That's a big gamble.

CH: Not really. Hunting Nick would have taken most of their resources, plus they'd need to know to go looking for him in the first place. We didn't see there being many other choices. We were out of options, but we'd taken measures to ensure we protected what we had.

DD: So extraction day arrived. And you're smiling.

CH: The extraction was in the middle of a field in Enfield. When we saw the chopper coming, everyone ran out from the hedge line, including Nick. We still hadn't had any contact with him, like I said, so it was a relief when we saw him running.

DD: And the other team?

CH: They were running too, but maybe not with as much energy as us. That's when I knew we'd won.

DD: How were they towards you?

CH: Pretty pissed, I think you can say.

DD: And Stacey in particular?

CH: Hard to tell.

DD: Why's that?

CH: She didn't acknowledge me. And before you ask, I was fine with that. It was a pretty childish reaction. The chopper landed and CAPOP jumped out, asked for the flags. Nick actually handed them to me.

DD: That was nice gesture.

CH: Yes. He was the only one to step forward. As soon as the flags were handed over, I asked CAPOP if there was any news on Homer. He shook his head. Stacey, in the meantime, started shouting that I'd stolen their flag. I remember the look in CAPOP's face, like he was just looking for an opportunity to annul the result, but he didn't.

        As the chopper took off with our team inside, I watched the others restraining Stacey as if she was going to try and grab the wheels.

DD: And?

CH: I haven't seen her since. I guess it will take her a long time to get back, but hopefully I'll get a chance to speak to her.

DD: If she remains in the process. Your group are the only ones guaranteed not to be culled. Do you feel anything about Stacey's reaction?

CH: Are you asking me if I will feel guilty if Stacey gets culled because I stole the flag from under her nose?

DD: Throughout this process you appear to have been essentially helping her through, especially in Evasion One. I don't know about the others, but this is the first time you've acted against her. It was the flag that you stole that ultimately won you the challenge and could lead her out of the course.

CH: So are you asking if I feel guilty?

DD: I'm not trying to put words in your mouth, but as you brought it up, do you feel any guilt?

CH: Yes, but not as much as I do for Homer.

[Silence]

DD: Could your guilt be one of the reasons why you stayed with her to have the coffee whilst she was on exercise? Perhaps you knew it might be the last opportunity before…

CH: Before she was gone. I guess it could have been.

[Silence]

DD: How does it feel to have won?

CH: We took off about two or three hours ago. I don't

think I've really processed. Still no one will tell me anything about Homer. I don't even know his real name and I'm not sure I did the right thing.

DD: Would you have given up if this was real? Would you have let yourself get captured just so you could know if he was okay?

CH: No.

DD: Then you did the right thing.

CH: But for the first time since forever, I asked myself if it was all worth it.

DD: And what was the answer?

CH: Is he dead?

DD: I didn't want to tell you anything until you had a chance to talk with me properly, but no. He's not dead. He is in a bad way and it is touch and go.

[Silence]

DD: Does that change anything?

CH: I should have done more to protect him.

DD: I'm not going to tell you if you made the right or wrong decision because I wasn't there. He is a volunteer. He joined the process. He knew what he was getting himself into. He made the choice despite your instructions.

CH: We could have found another way, but you're right. He made his choice and I made mine.

[Silence]

DD: Are you going home for Christmas?

[Silence]

CH: I've not really thought at the moment, but no. I'm staying here. I can't bring myself to go to my parents' house and be happy all over everyone. Saves me making up a load of...

[Silence]

CH: ...fantasy about what I've been doing since September.

DD: You don't need to tone down your language for me, Miss Hughes.

[Silence]

DD: You haven't spoken about your parents before. Do you get on with them?

CH: Doctor Devlin, do you mind if we pick this up next time? I would really like to be alone for a little while, if you don't mind.

DD: Go.

Journal of Dr Devlin, Head of Occupational Psychology

Section A ▮▮▮▮▮▮▮▮

8th December 2000 - Session 5.3

She's been hit hard by the incident with twenty-one, but in my view, it was an accident. I think she can take a little culpability but candidate twenty-one was told not to enter the premise.

Ms H's reaction to defer the decision to the group was both mature but also a sign of good leadership. She soon carried on making strong decisions once the group committed to continuing the challenge.

The act of candidate thirty-seven handing over the flags seemed to be the greatest gesture of respect which I don't think went unnoticed by Ms H.

I still feel that she is holding back in general, although other than her feelings for Stacey I cannot put my finger on which aspects in particular she is not opening up on.

When I told Ms H about twenty-one's condition, she gave no reaction, either to the fact that I knew and didn't tell her, or about him still being alive. She either really is the ice-cold bitch she professes to be, or she has an enormous amount of self-control. Because of her previous interactions when she was more relaxed, I believe it to be the former.

I'm concerned about Ms H's choice not to go home to her family for Christmas, but I feel it is part of her defence. Perhaps if she goes then comes back, she will relax too much and have to deal with everything that has gone on all over again. Although this will not affect her for the assessment, I feel she will need continually monitoring to protect her emotional health if she is successful in joining the organisation and continues to operate at the level she currently is.

TRANSCRIPT OF AUDIO RECORDING A1763529-1
[DEVICE C120 COVERT RECORDER]

[DATE: 24ᵗʰ JAN 2001] [14:01GMT]
[LOCATION: ▮▮▮▮▮▮▮▮▮▮▮▮▮▮▮▮▮▮▮▮▮*]*

DD: Just a short session today. I just wanted to see you before you head off on the final evasion exercise, and to wish you a happy birthday, of course.

CH: Thank you.

DD: I know it was a few weeks back, but…

CH: It's fine.

DD: How was Christmas?

CH: Great. Spent a week in bed.

DD: Were you ill?

CH: No. It was bliss. This place is a whole other world when all the candidates are gone.

DD: How so?

CH: Everyone turned human. There were a sizeable number of instructors still around, so they brought me in to bunk in their halls, along with another couple that hadn't gone home. We had Christmas lunch together, it was pretty neat.

DD: And now you're all best pals?

CH: *[Laughter]* No. They're back to normal now. Mean as hell again. How was your break, if I'm allowed to ask?

DD: It was fine, thank you. Did you get much reading done?

CH: *[Laughter]* Yes. I read *Goblet of Fire*, thank you, and I managed to get halfway through the copy of *IT*. I don't think I quite realised how little free time I'd have when I packed that one.

[Silence]

DD: I hear Homer is still the same.

CH: I didn't know that. They won't tell me. He's out of the process now. I don't think even the instructors know.

DD: How does that make you feel?

CH: I'm rationalising.

DD: How are you feeling with the next major assessment coming up? You must be pretty confident?

CH: I wouldn't say that. I've heard all about Tactical Questioning and all ten of us know what that's going to mean.

DD: Just ten of you left?

CH: Yeah, the last cull was deep. We'd been back from the short Christmas break for two days and they just walked the line, tapping shoulders and making people disappear.

DD: And you're on your own for this one.

CH: Yes. Stacey didn't come back after the urban exercise.

DD: Not even to get her things.

CH: No. Nothing.

DD: Did the rest of her team come back?

CH: Yes. I heard there was a fight as we flew away. One of the other team ended up with a broken arm. Stacey lost it, apparently.

DD: Did any of her team make it through?

CH: One of them did. Despite the broken arm, but he left in the last big cull.

DD: Do you think you'll see her again?

[Silence]

CH: Who knows.

[Silence]

CH: We didn't have a chance to say our goodbyes. No contact details.

[Silence]

CH: I don't even know her real name.

[Silence]

DD: Do you think she'll want to see you again?

CH: Once she's calmed down, I hope.

DD: There must be a pretty big hole in your life right now?

[Silence]

DD: Are you going to try and find her?

CH: I wouldn't be telling you if I was. Anyway, I've got more hell to go through first.

[Silence]

DD: What is it? Do you have something on your mind?

[Silence]

CH: I saw him.

DD: Please tell.

CH: On the operation. When I was sitting with Stacey having coffee.

DD: And you're only mentioning this now?

CH: I had other issues to deal with.

[Silence]

CH: He was maybe fifty metres from me.

[Silence]

CH: He stared back. I had a full, clear view. It was definitely me he was looking at and Stacey was sitting right next to me.

DD: That happened before?

CH: Yes, but this time she was staring right at him.

DD: And?

CH: She didn't see him. She said there was no one there.

[Silence]

DD: It's the stress. You'd better go. Oh, Miss Hughes.

[Silence]

DD: Good luck.

Journal of Dr Devlin, Head of Occupational Psychology

Section A ███████████

24th January 2001 - Session 6

Ms H seemed much more relaxed than when I saw her last, with an understandable reaction to the news, or no news, about candidate twenty-one.

She knows Stacey's real name. I can tell despite what she said, although I think it is only because she wanted me to know she knew her real name. I have the absolute belief that she could have kept that from me.

I wish I had time to explore the latest sighting. Even more so, if Stacey, candidate fifty-four, was still in the process. I'd have my colleague find out what she saw. But, alas, I'm not sure she would be too receptive to follow up questions if we could get in touch with her now.

TRANSCRIPT OF AUDIO RECORDING A1763529-1
[DEVICE C120 COVERT RECORDER]

[DATE:3rd FEB 2001] [17:09GMT]
[LOCATION: ███████████████████ *]*

DD: You did it.

CH: Did I?

DD: Well you made it this far. I'll be writing up my report and they'll make their decision by tomorrow morning. This is just a final chat to see where we are.

[Silence]

DD: Are you warm enough?

CH: Yes, I'm fine.

DD: You seem to be shivering.

CH: It's fine. Just my body relaxing.

[Silence]

DD: How was the interrogation? I mean Tactical Questioning.

CH: Awful.

DD: But you did well I hear?

CH: I didn't think you had access to that kind of operational information.

DD: I don't officially, but I kept an eye on you.

CH: I wouldn't say I did well.

DD: You got through it.

CH: Only because I knew they couldn't do any lasting damage, to my body anyway, although at the end there was more than a little doubt.

DD: What happened when you left this room?

CH: As soon as we were told to get dressed back in those World War Two cotton under-clothes and heavy wool coats, we knew it was time for the start of the hell.

[Silence]

DD: Carry on in your own time.

CH: I was expecting the format. They'd made a few changes to what I'd researched from SAS selection.

DD: Researched?

CH: SAS selection is well documented. There's even TV programmes about it.

DD: How did you know it would be anything like that?

CH: An educated guess. I had to start somewhere. If I was building a selection course then I would include it, weed out the weak minds. It works for the special forces.

DD: How was it different?

CH: During SF selection they have to stay out in the Brecons for a week, each day travelling a set distance, hitting checkpoints within certain times. They'd be equipped with a survival tin and a day's worth of water.
         They have two chances. If they get caught the second time, they're off the course. Seeking the help of anyone else would get you kicked off, but because there was a thousand-pound reward on their heads for any civilian giving them up, it made it an extremely risky option.

DD: I've heard stories in the past of operators staying the week with locals, some even set it all up weeks or months before the evasion element started. They'd be driven near to the checkpoint and picked up after they'd checked in.

CH: *[Laughter]* Sounds like bliss.

DD: And speaks volumes to their resourcefulness. How was this different?

CH: No checkpoints, just a precise area we had to stay in and a final destination to be at in a week's time, an area bounded by three major roads. Cross any of them and we were out. Again, with just the tin and a bottle of water, we were told we'd have an hour before the dogs were let loose.

DD: They turned their backs and started counting?

CH: Pretty much.

DD: And what did you do?

CH: What else was there to do? We ran. I was in a group of three and for the first half an hour we didn't speak. We were fuelled up and just ran in a straight line across fields and hills. We knew the best way to defeat the dogs would just be to get away as far as possible; the dogs and the handlers would tire with distance.

        At the first river we came to we just glanced at each other, the decision made without discussion. We knew we couldn't just cross; it would just enhance our smell, spraying our odour-laden droplets for the dog to pick up easily on the other side. Instead, we had to travel the river, slowing our progress, but making us less easy to track. So we believed.

DD: How long were you in the river for?

CH: About a kilometre, but we were in a shit state when we left. Those wool coats just soak up the water like a dry sponge.

DD: Wool is surprisingly good at keeping you warm when

it's wet.

CH: You know from personal experience?

DD: No.

[Silence]

CH: Our feet were soaked and we knew we couldn't wait too long to dry out. At least we'd got past what we agreed was the most dangerous part.

The sound of choppers came only moments after leaving the water, so we stuck to the tree canopy and just hoped they weren't using thermal imaging or there would be no point even bothering to wear ourselves out.

DD: And your companions? Did you think them more capable this time?

CH: Yes. This late on, the process had got rid of the chaff. I had Nick and one of his pals from the squadron with me, which gave me considerable relief. The constant banter helped to pass the time. Although I wasn't the only woman left in the final ten, they would take the piss out of me for not having a dick and I would constantly make references to what they would call their books when they failed, offering McNab's number if they wanted a leg up.

DD: You have McNab's number?

[Silence]

DD: Sorry, bad joke. How did they take it?

CH: Okay. I hadn't worked with the other guy that closely before. We'd been on day-long exercises together as a group and we'd seen each other around during the last six months of hell, but I could tell when we were first grouped together in that pub car park at the start he was sceptical of, of…

DD: He pre-judged you for being a woman?

CH: I know what you're going to say. Like I pre-judged the others on the London exercise.

[Silence]

CH: Anyway. Yes, but I threw that out of the window when I called them both cunts for not keeping up on the run up to the river. It seemed to settle him down. *[Weak laughter]* Anyway, we did our best to keep moving along the tree line, following the river as much as possible.

We found old bottles and flushed them through with river water, checking the next half mile for anything obvious dead upstream before we drank. We ended up stumbling upon a village as night started to fall. I say a village; it was less than that. What's the word? It had maybe a handful of houses and a post office, that's pretty much it.

DD: A hamlet?

CH: Yeah, that's the one. A hamlet. This place was tiny. Good news for us though, and surrounded by trees. We set a lay-up in a copse for us to regroup, well out of the way of any footpaths that seemed to be frequented by what was probably dog walkers and no doubt hikers in the season. We split to reccy the area and see what opportunities we could find.

DD: Did anyone take the lead?

CH: No. There seemed to be no need; we were all on the same wavelength.

Each of us headed in different directions, the other two fanning out closer to the outskirts of the hamlet while I went for higher ground to get a better picture of our surroundings. It wasn't long before I could hear voices ahead.

173

I took up a covered position, spotting three guys, probably early thirties, top to toe in Gucci hiking gear. They were making so much noise it made my job easy tracking them; their verbal diarrhoea was reminiscent of the two guys who'd just headed off in the opposite direction.

They were coming from the village, sorry hamlet. My thoughts were of the contents of their heavy packs, which I imagined were filled with kit and food that would make my life so much simpler. It was an easy decision to track them up the side of the small peak looming over us.

I didn't need to bother hiding my own noise; they were so loud and I followed them for a good half an hour before they decided to stop for a brew. In that moment, I took your advice.

DD: My advice?

CH: It was clear from the content of their conversations it was time to unleash my womanly charms.

DD: *[Laughter]* My role isn't training. *[Laughter]*

CH: Well, okay, let's just say you were the first to open up the possibility.

DD: I'm nervous to hear what you did. *[Laughter]*

CH: I waited for them to settle down, get the brew going on their little Swedish cookers. After ditching the thick wool coat, I just happened to stumble into their camp from the tree line.

DD: I bet their faces were a picture?

CH: You could say that. I just had those flimsy cotton trousers and khaki shirt on, the first few buttons must have slipped undone, damp water stains up my legs. They reeled back in horror at first, but they soon mellowed when they realised I wasn't some tramp about to nick their gear.

 After watching my fixed stare at the steam from their kettles, they asked me if I was okay and I knew I'd got them.

DD: They were definitely civilians?

CH: Yes, and pretty hardcore to be out at that time of the year. Or dumb.

DD: What did you tell them? Weren't you worried about the possibility of a reward on your head?

CH: It was a risk. I told them I couldn't say what I was doing, just that it was a training exercise and I was on the run.

DD: Did they buy it?

CH: They looked at each other. I could tell by their expressions they were thinking they would have known exactly what was going on if only I was a man. Other training exercises on those mountains are pretty famous, even for those who weren't from the area.

 A couple of the guys were from London, the other up north somewhere; Lancashire at a guess. Still they were quick to say they hadn't seen anyone around and thought I would be safe if I wanted to stop for a hot cup of tea. I made some coy comments about talking to strange men and it seemed to break the ice.

 I warned them I would be in a lot of trouble if I was seen with them. In the end I relented; the tea was supreme and the soup they gave me after was divine, even though I'd watched it poured from a packet. We chatted quietly. All the time I over-exaggerated my observations of the area, stopping the conversation each time there was a noise, out of place or not.

DD: And your womanly charms?

CH: I began to move closer into their circle, deliberately towards the one from London that seemed to have the nicest gear and was paying me the most attention. I steered the conversation to the nights ahead. They asked me where I'd stashed my kit and where my colleagues were. After telling them I was sitting in it and I was all alone until I was captured, their transformation was amazing.

        Each of them began rifling through their brightly-coloured rucksacks, pulling out clothes and dry bags. They clearly hadn't been in the military but were enthusiastic amateurs and seemed to have the right kit for the time of year.

        Despite my protests, I ended up with a pair of walking trousers, a thick green fleece, a dry bag full of chocolate, energy bars and a slip of paper with their numbers on. They offered for me to hide out with them in their three-man tent, saying I could trek alongside, blending in with their small party to keep me safe.

DD: Really?

CH: I'm not naive enough to think they weren't looking to get their rocks off, but they were acting really sweet and I was over the moon. I was, however, under no illusion; I had to get back to my team, but I couldn't leave them without a reward.

DD: Okay…

CH: I gave them each a hug and a kiss and told them I'd see them round. I'd call them when it was all over and return the gear. Which I meant. I'll have to replace it though; I'm not sure what those bastards did with it all.

DD: I wondered what you were going to say.

CH: Huh?

DD: Never mind. This is the first time I've heard you being anything but ambivalent to sex. How did that make you feel?

CH: Warm. It was so toasty that fleece.

DD: Not what I meant but carry on.

CH: I grabbed the new gear and left them to it, making as if I was heading back down.

DD: But you didn't?

CH: No. Once I'd disappeared over the small hill, I took myself back in the trees and got a good position where I could see them. Their banter seemed to have stopped; I think they were a bit shocked as they finished their tea in silence, but it all kicked off again as they moved away. Once they were well out of sight, I headed back through the trees, got my wool coat and skirted in a roundabout way back to the LUP.

DD: Were the others as successful?

CH: A box of eggs and a pint of milk that must have been left out all day.

DD: *[Laughter]*

CH: They were more than a little shocked to see me in my new threads under the wool coat, munching on a Snickers.

DD: I bet. Did it cause any friction between you?

CH: No, I shared out the food and it got me more than a little respect. We agreed to move further out from civilisation just in case those lads came across the hunters and inadvertently or otherwise gave away our position.

DD: You had a relatively easy time them?

CH: Day one maybe. It went downhill from there. We
        found another layup, rotating a watch each hour and
        I managed to get a few hours' sleep. There were
        moments when I felt a little guilty; I was freezing cold
        and had some proper clothes on, the other two were
        in a much worse state, but I'd done the work and the
        prize was mine.
                The first fright came at dawn. I woke when
        one of the guys thought they spotted a section of
        hunters piling from a truck on a remote road maybe
        a couple of kilometres away. We knew it wouldn't be
        long before the choppers would be hitting the air
        again.
                We spent the rest of the day constantly on
        our heels, trying not to get too close to the RV point,
        which was only about forty K from our position,
        knowing it would be swamped with hunters, but at
        the same time knowing that the hunters were at our
        backs. They either knew our location or were at least
        trying to herd us in the direction we weren't ready to
        go.

DD: But they didn't get you.

CH: Sure, but they kept the pace up so high we were
        exhausted by the fourth day and now one of the guys
        carried an injury. A twisted ankle that slowed us right
        down.

DD: Nick?

CH: No. Tom.

DD: Was this a team exercise?

CH: We couldn't really tell. Yes, we headed out in small
        groups and if it was real we would have stayed
        together as much as we could.

DD: Would you?

CH: Well, depending on the reason we were out in the middle of nowhere, running away from a hunter force hell bent on capture or worse. I guess if we had something, some piece of information we had to get into friendly hands then no, we wouldn't have let the slow man dictate the pace.

DD: But you did?

CH: For a while. I took the alternative view after another day. We didn't argue, we just agreed that the guys would stay together. Their code wouldn't let them separate and I would make my own way. What was the point in us all failing just because of one miss-step? Don't you think?

DD: You should know by now it doesn't matter what I think. You had your reasons.

[Silence]

DD: In the end they must have split as Tom came in a couple of days before you both.

CH: I think I was right to make the decision early on.

[Silence]

CH: For the good of the objective.

DD: So how was it being alone?

CH: I didn't sleep as much. It's not true you can sleep with one eye open. I tried. I'd either bury myself in the under growth, covering up under stinking half-decayed leaves, which are surprisingly warm, or lean against a tree, where I could find them dense enough, but I'd always wake as I fell backwards, or heard a noise.

DD: But you got through it.

CH: And I think that was a mistake. I should have realised
        they were lying. It didn't matter if you got to the end.
        It only mattered that you'd not slept properly for four
        or more days. I should have just stayed in the same
        place, somewhere really good to hide, then given up.

DD: I don't understand.

CH: You can't appreciate what it's like not to have slept for
        six days, not to have eaten properly for the same.
        Those chocolate bars were gone too quickly and the
        little amounts of water I was drinking from streams
        was playing havoc with my stomach.
              It hit me as I was in the Land Rover having
        crossed the finish line. The warmth was suffocating;
        I couldn't close my eyes I was so on edge. Colours
        were wrong. I was hallucinating. I was seeing things
        and hearing things that weren't there. If they'd have
        dressed up as the Mad Hatter from *Alice in
        Wonderland,* I would have given them everything there
        and then.

DD: Only half the group made it to the finish line, only
        another two passed the four-day mark. That's an
        achievement.

CH: I'll pat myself on the back when this is all over. At the
        moment I'm just glad I'm done. I should have lasted
        longer under interrogation; two days wouldn't be
        enough time for a rescue force to find me.

DD: You wouldn't have any idea of what the time was
        while you were in there, surely?

CH: I didn't, but I should have lasted longer until I spilled
        my guts.

DD: You miss the point. No one would be able to hold out
        indefinitely. The key is to keep the slow trickle of

information coming, making yourself more valuable with your heart still pumping. What did you tell them?

CH: Everything. The route I'd taken, my name and that I'm a bad person in training.

DD: *[Laughter]* That's nothing.

CH: It's what they wanted so I shouldn't have given it to them.

DD: Two days is a long time in anyone's books. The guy who lasted the longest, he'd been through it in real life; he has the scars across his back to prove it. He only lasted a couple of hours longer before he was spilling his life story. You only revealed short term operational information, he was singing about real operations conducted last year.

CH: Maybe I knew it didn't matter.

DD: I get that and that's why you won. To everyone else it was as real as it gets and these guys should know.

CH: I don't think I'd cope if it was real.

DD: Tell me about it. Tell me the worst.

[Silence]

CH: The first part was as expected.

DD: Expected?

CH: I knew about the sensory deprivation. A bag on the head which after a couple of hours makes you see and hear things that aren't there. I'd already started from that point. You hear the sound of breath, of panting, of panic. Then comes the white noise, with an interlude of heavy metal so loud you can't think.

[Silence]

DD: We can take a break here if you need to?

[Silence]

CH: After a while you dial it out and concentration switches to the pain of squatting with your hands tied at your back.

[Silence]

CH: You try to make micro movements in a vain attempt to fend off the cramps. Sorry I've got to stand up.

DD: Please do.

CH: As you start to control yourself in a kind of meditation, the music and white noise stop, like they know exactly what's going on in your head.

There's a huge void in the information you're getting from your senses. You hear movement around you, then a shout by your ear, the words unintelligible. Soon you can't tell if it's real or it didn't happen at all. Your body convulses with the energy from an unexpected dog's bark.

[Silence]

CH: The white noise would start and you'd ask yourself what was coming next. The supply of adrenalin would slow and the pain in your legs would be back twice as sharp. The second time the sound stopped I smelt the dogs before I heard their snarls and their claws scratching at the tiled floor, eager to tear flesh.

I lost count of the rounds, five or six at a guess and still each time I would fall for the lull, even though I knew it was only temporary. I was exhausted and starving; I hadn't eaten for two days before I was captured.

[Silence]

DD: I can get you something to eat if you like?

CH: Not yet. Thank you.

[Silence]

CH: Once when the sound went off, a hand violently shook at my shoulder. I heard my scream and the muffled cries of a little girl. I stopped only as the comfort of the white noise began assaulting my ears again. It hit me harder than I'd expected.

I was so disappointed in myself. They'd already broken me down. I hadn't cried like that since I was a young child. I hadn't cried during this entire shitty process, but now I had tears streaming down my face.

I was still in shock when a hand covered my mouth and I was pulled by the shoulders and on to a stretcher or something and carried off, the stretcher running left and right almost jerking me to the floor several times. My bound hands were pushing into the middle of my back, my shoulders screaming to take away the pressure and dislocate.

We stopped somewhere, where I had no clue; there was no chance of tracing the route, even if I'd had the mental energy to try. I lay there for an age. Each time I tried to move I was pushed back on to my throbbing shoulders. Even through the pain I found myself drifting to sleep, but was jolted side to side and dropped heavily to the floor, jerking awake.

DD: Take a minute if you need it.

CH: Sorry. I want to get this done. I want to move on and never think about it again.

[Silence]

DD: It's healthy to talk about it. Trust me.

CH: I'll take your word for it.

[Silence]

CH: Hands grappled me to my feet; it felt like my muscles
        were tearing from the bone as I stretched out my
        limbs that had been cramped for so long. Eventually
        I was pushed into a seat, the bag ripped from my
        head, light screaming at me from two bright spots
        ahead.
                I felt myself resigned; I was ready to give in.
        I'd decided maybe life as an accountant or a bin man
        wouldn't be so bad after all, but as the unseen guy's
        words carried along the table, my preparation started
        to come back and with it, a few precious drops of
        resolve.

DD: What did they ask you?

CH: They asked me who I was. I'd drawn up a plan long
        ago in my head. I'd prepared my story; it was how I'd
        spent my time out on exercise in the cold or any
        moment I had free, comforting myself that as I lay
        shivering to try and sleep, with one ear open for any
        noise, I knew it would be so much worse when I was
        captured.
                I wasn't wrong. My throat was dry and all I
        could do was mouth the words. I was telling them
        everything, my prepared story, each word formed
        slowly and with perfect grace, just with the lack of
        sound as it refused to come out of my throat.

DD: Was the silence part of the plan?

CH: No.

DD: Weren't you worried you would frustrate them?

CH: I had no choice and they tried to talk me round. They
        tried being nice at first, offering coffee and cigarettes;
        I accepted the first. Even though the words were lost,
        I kept going and when I came to the end, I started
        from the beginning.
                The interrogator soon tired and was up in my

face. He smoked; his breath stank. I concentrated on that stench. As he shouted and screamed at me, I thought of him going home to his wife and kids. I thought of him making love to his wife, being gentle as he said goodnight to his children, his screamed words no longer registering.

My research told me to concentrate on a spot, to keep something visually locked or to think of anything in your mind but your family; something else, didn't matter what, just lock yourself into it.

DD: What did you think about?

[Silence]

CH: I couldn't do as I prepared. Instead, I imagined him as a person outside of this torture. I barely registered his venom increase, only noticing as more of his spit hit my face with each shout. He couldn't keep it up; it felt like a victory as I was hooded and carted in reverse back to the white noise.

The second time was a much shorter stint, two cycles I think before I gave my little scream and the signal I was duly softened again. I repeated the process with a different instructor and each time I could hear their frustration build. Hour upon hour they would up the volume, building until…

[Silence]

DD: Keep going please, no matter how hard it seems.

[Silence]

CH: Until for the first time I felt a sharp sting across my face, forcing a mistake. The slap rattled me out of my safe place. I was shocked and I let it tell. They had been working on trying to do exactly this, but with words. Now with a simple administration of pain they could get what they wanted. I told them my name.

I realised I'd done wrong, clamming up tight and they carted me back to the white noise, cursing myself for their first success.

On the third round I lasted the most, eight cycles, which I convinced myself was a major victory, despite wetting myself in the process, but I let that slip. We'd been given as much water as we dared to drink when we were picked off the moors and I'd guzzled like a new born on its mother's tit.

[Silence]

CH: Back in the darkened interrogation room, the air smelt so fresh when they took the hood off and I realised that if there were any others left in that holding room with me, they'd not let any of them use the toilet either. There was no mucking around this time. The lights were low and I could see her face clear as I can see yours.

DD: Was this the first female interrogator?

CH: Yes, and she didn't beat around the bush, asking me if I knew I was adopted. I remember stopping in my tracks, my mind freezing for a moment as I struggled with her words. She repeated herself and I willed myself to ignore her, but try as I might, I couldn't get the same comforting narrative running in my head.

[Silence]

CH: You look surprised.

DD: I didn't know you were adopted. There's nothing in your personnel records.

CH: Neither did I.

[Silence]

DD: I'm not sure what to say. I suggest you continue.

CH: She asked me if I knew I'd been brought up by imposters.

DD: This is the first time I've seen you get angry when talking to me.

CH: She took care to form each of the words, making sure I couldn't mistake anything I was hearing. She let me sit in silence; no doubt she could tell I was processing my thoughts, trying to figure out if it was a ploy or if they had their nails in a crack.

I actually began to analyse. Were my looks the same as my sister's? Her hair was blonde, her eyes blue, her height below mine by a few inches. Then I thought about each of my parents; their features were no match for either of us children. Maybe we were both adopted from different families?

She interrupted my train of thought, bringing out documents, one of which I recognised as a birth certificate; the browning, almost parchment-like page with the red frame of an official notice. She started reading aloud my life story, the hospital I was born in, the date I came into this world, but then she read two names I wasn't familiar with. Names I'd never heard.

She shoved the page in front of me, swapping out the other over the top. That was *my* birth certificate. That was my name. My first name.

Still, I wasn't convinced. The piece of paper did nothing; well, maybe offer a little doubt. You used to be called ▮▮▮, she said, but my happy place was already coming back, faltering every so often as I caught the odd sentence while she read from a three page report about my real parents, my smack-head of a mother who died only three years after my birth and my father whose file was too big to fit through the door to the room.

[Silence]

DD: Take your time.

CH: What really caught me off guard was when she used
       my real name.

[Silence]

CH: She started asking me if I'd met my father, asking me
       if I'd had contact because she knew he wanted to,
       knew he'd tried so hard in the past. I wanted to ask
       questions, wanted to find out if she was saying what
       I thought she had meant, but I knew to start the
       conversation would have split me open; anything they
       wanted would spill out.
              She insisted all I needed to do was tell them
       my number and all would be over. Tell them what I
       was doing out on the moor and I could walk away
       unharmed. They'd add in the address of my real dad
       if I wanted to get in touch. She pulled out a picture
       of my sister and held it beside my face. She didn't say
       anything, just squinted and ushered herself away.

[Silence]

CH: In that moment I had no idea what was real and what
       was made up. I started to believe what she was saying.
       She started screaming my old name at me. It was too
       much, but rather than going in further, I was dragged
       away and back on my feet, setting into the crouch that
       despite their best efforts my muscles were kind of
       used to.
              Even with the hood I knew the room was
       different, damp, but clean smelling and smaller, the
       white noise bouncing off the walls, the bass of the
       heavy drums echoing against the thick hood. All I
       could think of was the stupid story, doubts looming
       over me. I wanted to speak with the people who
       brought me up, my parents, real or not, for them to
       reassure me it was all lies.

A scream cut through the noise, clear as day above the cacophony, but it was so strong, so exaggerated, so unreal I assured myself it was just a part of the recording. The screams added as time went on; they were the same and so obviously unreal, but still I felt myself wince when I thought about what or who had made them.

Something new was soon added to the mix, another noise and a feeling as I moved my feet. On the floor was water, but not from me; I hadn't had enough liquid in my body for some time and the smell was fresh and clean.

Time went on along with the din and I zoned out, trying to think my way out of the room, but when I shifted my feet in an attempt to calm the tightness, I felt a cold sting at my ankles.

DD: Was it pain?

CH: No, it was a new sensation. Water.

[Silence]

CH: The white noise cut and I struggled to move my feet, but as I did, I heard the water move and lap at my ankles and I thought oh shit.

Now I concentrated on the rise. It was slow but measured. The noise was gone and I was just left with the slow lapping of tiny waves against the walls. Sooner than I'd have liked, I felt the cold wetness above my ankles and I took a sharp breath as the cold stung at my crotch.

As it first touched my hands I knew if I fell either forward or back, I wouldn't be able to easily get my head above the water.

I was trying to concentrate on things I could do when this was all over. Meet up with my sister, my parents, go out for a meal and sit in some country pub, warming my hands on a fire. I thought of finding Stacey, going out for lunch, having coffee without having to look over my shoulder. I'd even go on that dreaded shopping trip she'd been insisting we'd take, spending some time in normality.

I heard another voice, this time deep, but calm in my ear.

DD: What did it say?

CH: 'Are you okay?' it said. It sounded a bit like you until it turned to laughter. I felt like screaming as the laughter continued, my hands immersed and freezing. I wanted to tell all; I'd had enough, but I was really worried my voice wouldn't hold out.

I felt a sharp hit at both shoulders and I tumbled backwards. My instinct made me pull in breath just before I hit the water. My head was under and I was wriggling around, trying to turn to get to my knees and pull my head up, but all I managed was to thrash with no focus.

I felt the water surge away as if someone had opened a wide dam, gravity returned to normal and I lay my head against the freezing cold concrete, panting for air.

[Silence]

CH: I was left there for less than a minute before my arms were pulled up against my shoulders and I was on my feet, led somewhere unknown as I concentrated on the thought of the soaking-wet trail I was leaving down the corridor.

There were no bright lights as they pulled the hood and the cuffs released. My eyes quickly became used to the dull illumination on the chair opposite me across from the table as I rotated my arms to ease my stiff shoulders. I hadn't seen the woman of around thirty who sat opposite me before.

I was trying to be weary of the kindest smile

I'd seen in some time, but my defences fell when she pushed over a cup of coffee she'd just poured. I drank the whole cup down. It was delicious; a welcome assault on my senses. She poured another. I knew I would think different in an hour or so, but now I was living for each little mercy in whatever form it came.

[Silence]

DD: Are you warm enough? I can get a blanket if you need.

CH: No. Thank you. I think it's just my body remembering. She refused to pour a fourth cup, telling me I should let the first three go down. I started to sob; kindness was the cruellest of their weapons, as I knew she was just giving light so that the later dark would be that much more powerful.

She was the good cop and any minute something bad would happen to catch me off guard, but I was hooked and along for the ride.

She stooped to her side and pulled overalls from the floor, stood and pressed the dry uniform into my hands and moved around the table, turning away. I stood, shaking, water spraying the floor as I moved to the corner, peeling off my soaking clothes. I was completely naked, hopping from one foot to the next to keep warm; it wasn't cold in the room but I was saturated and covered in goose bumps.

I threw the soaked clothes into a pile in the opposite corner. Lights sprung on, two pointed directly at me as I turned, another shining at the back of the room and six faces, including the woman's, each wearing a sickly leering grin.

I hurried my leg into the jump suit, but my heart sank to find they'd sown the legs up, the arms too.

They'd won. I couldn't bear to put the

soaking clothes back on. I walked back naked and sat down at the table, pouring myself another cup as I told them my name was Corra Hughes and I was out on the moor because I'm training for something, but I have no idea what.

DD: I feel like clapping.

[Silence]

DD: You were amazing.

[Silence]

DD: I don't have to tell you that.

[Silence]

CH: It doesn't feel like a victory.

DD: You know it had to seem real, don't you?

CH: Of course, but I shouldn't have let it get to me.

DD: It was always going to get to you. That's the point. No one gets to the end. The interrogators will just carry on and it will get harder and harder.

CH: I should have lasted longer.

DD: Remember, it's not just a selection course, it's training, too. An experience you hopefully will never have to draw on and you didn't give up. You were subjected to over forty-seven hours of extreme stress. They broke the law in every western country and if this was a conflict situation, the Geneva Convention would be in tatters.

CH: But I'm a volunteer.

DD: And prepared.

CH: Prepared for what?

192

DD: Now you survived that, if you're ever in the same situation again, you stand a chance of a rescue team getting to you in time. I think I'm not speaking out of turn to tell you that they would be out of their minds not to come to the right decision tomorrow.

But you're right, what you experienced was nothing compared to a real situation. We know that it would most likely be worse, there'd be pain and torture, scars that would never properly heal. The only question left is do you still want to change your life forever?

[Silence]

CH: Yes.

Journal of Dr Devlin, Head of Occupational Psychology

Section A ████████████

3ʳᵈ February 2001 - Session 7

It would appear that Ms H was able to deploy her charms during the exercise. I feel a little guilty that I put the suggestion into her head, but I also know she is more than capable of making the decision and protecting herself if matters didn't turn out quite so well as they did.

We have made great progress. Ms H shared the food she was given by the hikers. This experience seems to have rounded off some of the edges of her sharp personality.

It is always difficult to listen to the candidates recount the interrogation phase. Despite her fears, she did extremely well, especially when they introduced the issue relating to the adoption. I still am unclear as to whether this whole aspect is a tactic by the interrogation team or not. Ms H clearly took some store in the issue and as I commented back to her, she became visibly angry when she first recounted the interrogator's words. It barely needs saying but it certainly took her by surprise and the details they provided were at a level that were difficult to dismiss without further investigation.

I have written up my recommendations and, along with the rest of her assessment, I have no doubt Ms H will be joining us for the foreseeable future. I genuinely look forward to our sessions when she is operational.

TRANSCRIPT OF AUDIO RECORDING A1763529-1
[DEVICE C120 COVERT RECORDER]

[DATE: 4th FEB 2001]
[LOCATION: 52.97865, -3.64134]

[Period of muffled voices followed by a long silence]

CH: Bollocks. Again?

[Silence]

CH: Really?

[Silence]

CH: I knew I shouldn't have listened to that bloody shrink.
         You guys are a joy.

[Identified as James Doran (JD), Former Instructor (Discharged(D) 2000), Section E ███████████████████]

JD: *[Laughter]* Think of it as an added bonus.

CH: *[Sarcastically]* Just for me?

[Silence]

CH: And the hood, again really?

[Silence]

CH: Can you loosen these straps? My hands are going
         numb?

[Light footsteps]

JD: They feel fine.

CH: You're the one from… *[Laughter]* Makes sense. I
         thought you were fired.

JD: You recognise my voice?

CH: And that same stink from your dirty laundry.

195

JD: I'd steer off the conversation if I were you.

CH: I guess. Where are we?

JD: Where do you think we are?

CH: I have a bag on my head, so no bloody idea. I guess it's not the training centre.

[Silence]

CH: Did you drug me? My head feels like shit.

JD: I could apologise, but I'm not going to.

CH: Okay. What's the deal then?

JD: I understand you pretty much aced the selection process, so well done for that.

CH: Thanks, but I asked what's going on now?

JD: Don't be impatient, we have plenty of time. This is all about exploring your options.

CH: Is this some sort of tripped out job fair?

JD: *[Laughter]* You could say that, but there's only one job on offer.

CH: Okay, I'm confused. I wouldn't mind cutting to the chase. What are these options?

JD: There's only one other option.

CH: I'm not sure I'm on the same page.

JD: Let's just say this is where the real job opportunity comes to light.

CH: Finally, I get to know what this job is all about?

JD: Hold that thought. Do you know who was running the process you've just been through?

CH: You're talking like you don't.

JD: Oh, believe me I know who they are. You clearly don't know the details of the role, but do you at least know who you were going to work for?

CH: So I take it you are not them…

[Silence]

CH: …they, whichever it is?

JD: Spot on. Do you know who they are?

CH: No.

[Silence]

CH: Not a clue. I was hoping I'd find out tomorrow, if I passed, of course.

JD: Today now and you would have passed.

CH: Would have? What do you mean?

JD: I'm afraid they'll no longer be seeking your services.

CH: What?

JD: Because you went missing before they could offer you the job.

CH: Sorry am I being obtuse here? What the hell are you talking about?

JD: The organisation wasn't military; you know that much. It wasn't even a government department. It's not even privately owned, really.

CH: So?

JD: It's a self-funding organisation of vigilantes. They go about righting wrongs and telling everyone they dare to speak to how much of a good job they do.

CH: And they don't do a good job?

JD: Depends on your definition of good.

CH: I guess that depends on your perspective.

JD: You got it.

CH: And your perspective is different to theirs.

JD: You're a fast learner all right. I bet you get told that all the time.

CH: I do. It's annoying, isn't it?

JD: Not at all. Makes my job that bit easier.

[Silence]

CH: Your organisation has a different point of view. Doesn't that make you the bad guys?

JD: In their eyes, I guess. Most people are defined by a moral code and for the majority of those on the planet those morals are aligned, but there are more than a few overlaps here and there. Like child brides, for example.

CH: I get it.

JD: Let me finish. To most people the justification for killing someone is pretty high, let's say murder or rape in some countries, really serious stuff. But what about if someone brings down a bank and forces governments to go bankrupt?
        What if stopping them quite literally dead could save the suffering of hundreds or thousands, if not more?
        Who gets to choose?
        What if you sold arms so a country could defend itself against an aggressor, then someone sells arms to the other side, convinced it is they that have

198

SECRET – WHEN REDACTED

been wronged?

CH: I understand your point. It's an age-old argument that I'm sure is discussed in many a social studies classroom across the globe.

JD: Watch your attitude.

CH: You try sitting here with this bag on your head.

JD: Fucking listen.

CH: I'm listening.

JD: What I'm trying to explain is that you should be able to understand that the organisation I work for has a different point of view from the organisation you were about to join.

CH: Look, I understand, but remind me why I'm here with a bag on my head?

JD: *[Laughter]* We've been watching you.

CH: That's not creepy in the slightest.

JD: You've been highlighted to us as someone who could potentially join our organisation.

CH: Who highlighted me?

JD: That's irrelevant, for now.

CH: Let me get this straight. You want to offer me a job, so you kidnap me and shove me in restraints.

JD: We know from experience that you may not be in the right frame of mind to immediately come to the mutually beneficial decision we need to achieve.

CH: *[Laughter]* This is a joke, of course, *[Laughter]* or another test. It has to be. *[Laughter, clears throat]* So I get to stay here until I decide to join you?

JD: This is not a joke, I assure you, and your stay is not
         indefinite. There is a time window.

CH: And in that time you get to put your case?

JD: That's right.

CH: Okay, let's get started. How are we going to do this?

JD: Now that would be telling. Let's just say we're going
         to be very compelling.

CH: You got me already. I'll join. I'm all yours. Undo my
         wrists and I'll go get my things from my bunk and I'll
         be back to join the forces of evil so we can start with
         the training. There is training, right?

JD: There's no need to be like that. I understand you still
         think this is part of the process. Classic behaviour,
         I'm afraid. We'll need to get you into a more
         productive frame of mind.

CH: Okay.

JD: We've tried many ways in the past, but have found
         there is one sure-fire way that gets by far the most
         results.

CH: How long have you been doing this?

[Chair scrapes against the floor]

CH: This is ten…

[Dull thud and heavy out breath]

CH: What the fuck? Oh my god. I believe you, I believe
         you.

JD: Sorry but…

[Dull thud and heavy out breath]

CH: Fuuuuck!

200

JD: Don't try and talk. Give yourself a moment to get your breath back and just think about what I said.

[Silence]

JD: Your face is pretty bloody hard.

[Slow intake of breath]

JD: I would get you something for the swelling, but that's kind of the point. Just sit back and let me tell you all about what we do here.

CH: *[Muffled grunt]*

[Dull thud and heavy out breath]

JD: Quietly.

[Silence]

JD: We're pretty much the same as the other guys. We sneak around, getting information from people who don't want to give it. We find people that don't want to be found, we help protect our clients from nasty people, organisations and governments and we take people out of situations to stop bad things happening.

         Both of the organisations are in the same market scale; mega corporations, governments, trading blocs often, but those guys have a very narrow focus. We, on the other hand, have the whole world as our market.

CH: You do this for money.

JD: As do they, but they have only one customer, whereas we are a commercial operation.

CH: For whoever has the money.

JD: Not whoever. You should listen to what I say. Look, we all have the same basic set of morals, just a few overhang at the edges.

CH: Beating a hooded woman in the face is an overhang?

JD: Don't think they wouldn't. Our methods aren't too different.

CH: Cut to the chase. If I don't join, you kill me?

JD: You're a quick learner; they were right about you. If we don't get you, we can't have you working against us.

CH: Why do you think I would even consider your offer after what you just did?

JD: It's an interesting one, I know. One of the physiologists tried to explain it, but in the end, I gave up trying to understand. All you need to know is that there will be a point in this process where you have to make that decision. You have to decide whether it's something you want to do for the rest of your life or lose what life you have left.

        You will make that decision. We have some very compelling arguments.

CH: You've done this before then.

JD: As I say, we're well practiced.

CH: If you keep grabbing their best candidates, aren't you worried they'll come after you?

JD: They'd have to find us first.

[Silence]

CH: Can we get on with it?

JD: As you wish.

[Silence, punctuated with the infrequent turning of paper]

CH: What are you doing?

202

JD: Research.

[Silence, punctuated with the infrequent turning of paper]

JD: How's the ankle?

CH: Holding up well.

JD: Good.

[Silence, punctuated with the infrequent turning of paper]

JD: A turbulent childhood.

CH: Huh?

[Silence, punctuated with the infrequent turning of paper]

JD: What do you think he would have done to you if he'd have got hold of you?

CH: *[Inaudible]* If you read on, you'll find out.

JD: *[Laughter]* I wondered when the penny would drop. It makes an interesting read.

[Chair legs scrape against the floor] [Door hinges squeal]

CH: Are you there?

[Silence, then door hinges squeal] [Chair legs scrape against the floor]

JD: *[Laughter]* It would be funny if he worked for them.

[Laughter]

CH: Funnier still if he worked for you.

JD: *[Laughter]* Wouldn't it? Shame we didn't start looking at you until you were at Welbeck.

[Silence, punctuated with the infrequent turning of paper]

JD: Ah, Stacey. We'll get to her.

[Silence]

JD: I wouldn't bother doing that, you'll just make your wrists sore.

[Silence, punctuated with the infrequent turning of paper]

JD: You know they actually took the money you stole from my car out of my wages.

[Silence, punctuated with the infrequent turning of paper]

JD: Wow, Welbeck. The Chadwick Challenge.

[Silence]

JD: That was you?

[Silence]

JD: You getting this? We've got a fucking celebrity in our midst.

[Silence]

JD: This day just got a whole lot better. *[Laughter]*

CH: I'll sign it for you if you want?

JD: *[Laughter]*

[Silence, punctuated with the infrequent turning of paper]

JD: And it begins.

CH: Is he working for you?

JD: Which one?

CH: Devlin.

JD: I'm afraid I don't have access to that kind of operational information. *[Laughter]*

[Silence, punctuated with the infrequent turning of paper]

JD: You're a serious bitch.

CH: And you're a slow reader.

JD: You've read the manual. Stay on my good side.

[Silence, punctuated with the infrequent turning of paper]

JD: A people magnet. Figures.

[Silence, punctuated with the infrequent turning of paper]

JD: I like the way this is going. He's good.

[Silence, punctuated with the infrequent turning of paper]

JD: Sword   of   Honour.   *[Sarcastic   laughter]*   In   my
        experience, most people that win are troublemakers
        and leave as soon as they've done their three years.
        They go off to the city and burn through other
        people's money.

CH: Didn't win then?

[Silence, punctuated with the infrequent turning of paper]

JD: A kiss from the lovely Stacey. Lucky girl.

[Silence, punctuated with the infrequent turning of paper]

JD: I deliberately left the car open.

CH: I'm sure.

[Silence, punctuated with the infrequent turning of paper]

[Dull thud and heavy out breath]

CH: Fuck sake. Not my fucking feet please.

[Dull thud and heavy out breath]

CH: Sorry, you don't have the manners of a monkey.

[Silence, punctuated with the infrequent turning of paper]

JD: And we get to the juicy bits.

205

CH: How predictable.

JD: Shush.

[Silence, punctuated with the infrequent turning of paper]

JD: I'm getting a boner.

CH: Pleased for you.

JD: You will be. Or not.

[Silence]

JD: He goes into a lot of specifics though, doesn't he?

[Silence, punctuated with the infrequent turning of paper]

JD: Wow, a virgin. Now I'm getting properly hard. Are you really still a virgin?

[Silence]

JD: You're right not to answer. I'll have more fun finding out for myself.

[Silence, punctuated with the infrequent turning of paper]

JD: And you like the ladies. Shit this stuff is gold dust. He's so flirting with you.

CH: He wasn't.

JD: Whoa. You liked him?

CH: I thought he was a nice guy, in the end.

JD: Did you want to fuck him?

CH: No. One of the advantages of not having a cock for a brain.

JD: We'll see.

CH: You know he's gay, don't you?

206

[Silence]

JD: Not surprised he's a faggot to be fair.

[Silence, punctuated with the infrequent turning of paper]

JD: *[Laughter]* You got one right over that bloody
          ███████. CAPOP was such a fucking Hitler. I'd
          love to get him in this room.

CH: Would you talk dirty to him too?

JD: *[Laughter]* My cock's just for the ladies. I should let
          you go just for what you did to him.

[Silence, punctuated with the infrequent turning of paper]

JD: Just to be clear, I'm not going to.

[Silence, punctuated with the infrequent turning of paper]

JD: Interesting.

[Silence, punctuated with the infrequent turning of paper]

JD: Oh, how nice, you didn't want me to get in trouble.

[Silence, punctuated with the infrequent turning of paper]

JD: I take that back.

[Silence, punctuated with the infrequent turning of paper]

JD: *[Laughter]* You're so right about Mel. *[Laughter]*

[Silence, punctuated with the infrequent turning of paper]

JD: He used to freak the shit out of me too, I know what
          you mean.

[Silence]

JD: *[Laughter]* Tom, brilliant.

[Silence, punctuated with the infrequent turning of paper]

207

JD: Poor Mike.

CH: Huh?

JD: That was the guy's name. The guy you got, sorry, that got run over by the police car.

[Silence]

JD: You were right though; you should have gone to him straight away. Maybe never left him on his own.

CH: Old news. I'm over it.

JD: He's not. Lost both his legs. He's in a wheelchair now, but look on the bright side…

CH: The bright side?

JD: At least he's got a shot at the Paralympics. *[Laughter]*

CH: You're so funny. I wanna join now.

[Silence]

CH: Tell me, is there a stage somewhere, near the bar in your social club maybe, where you get to stand in front of all the others and tell them all your amazing jokes?

JD: Keep quiet, bitch, or you might find a matching bruise on the other side.

[Silence, punctuated with the infrequent turning of paper]

JD: Did you like getting your kit off in front of all those guys?

CH: I think they got more of a kick out of it than I did.

JD: If that was a real situation, they'd probably tag team you till you're bleeding from all of your holes.

[Silence]

208

JD: I bet that'll convince you this is real.

[Silence]

JD: *[Laughter]* Now you're keeping quiet.

[Silence, punctuated with the infrequent turning of paper]

JD: Shall I get the lads in and we can give it whirl?

CH: Do we really need all of them? I've no experience so
          I'm sure you'll be man enough for me. Untie me and
          I can find out what all the fuss is about?

[Silence]

JD: *[Laughter]* Cheap. I thought better of you, but don't
          worry, it won't be too long before you'll know what it
          feels like to have a man buried deep inside you. I have
          a feeling we're going to need plenty of lube.

CH: I don't know, the hood, the leather around my wrists,
          some people find that pretty sexy.

[Silence]

CH: Do you?

[Chair legs scrape against the floor]

[Silence]

CH: You want some?

[Silence]

CH: Any chance you could take a shower before we do
          this? You fucking stink.

[Sudden outpour of breath]

CH: *[Strained words]* Guess not. *[Heavy breath]* We should
          go out for a drink first, get to know each other a little
          better.

[Silence]

CH: I warn you I'm desperate for a piss.

[Silence]

CH: Why don't you take this hood off and I'll see what I can do for you? I won't bite it off, I promise.

[Ripping material] [Door hinges squeal] [Chair scrapes against the floor]

[Silence]

CH: Was it getting a bit hot for him?

[Identified as Fiona Dervish (FD), ███████ ████████ ████████ █ ███████████████████ *]*

FD: How did you know...?

[Silence]

FD: It was his break.

CH: Just as I was getting in the mood.

FD: Yeah.

[Silence]

FD: Where did he get to?

CH: It was your perfume, light as it is. It's better than his BO. It made me thankful for this rotten hood. Plus, you're a lot lighter than him. Your footsteps, I mean. How do they train you guys?

[Silence, punctuated with the infrequent turning of paper]

CH: This was my favourite top.

[Silence, punctuated with the infrequent turning of paper]

FD: At least we know how to get to you. Shall we start with a stress position again?

CH: Happy to oblige, but that's been done. I reckon I could outlast the time you've got for me.

FD: I feel you may be right, but this seems a good a time to clarify something. Your attitude, while laudable, gives us the impression you think we need you to cooperate, more than we need you to. We know either way that you'll not be working against us at the end of this, and *[laughter]* you're not the only member of this year's intake that showed promise.

        In fact, next door we have another who is making much better progress. That's maybe because she doesn't start with the same options you did.

CH: Let me guess. You're reading the transcripts of Dr Devlin's recordings, so… Stacey?

FD: Oopsey, there goes the suspense. Did I make it that obvious?

[Silence]

FD: I must remember to tone it down a bit next time. My bad.

CH: Why the fuck are you getting her involved? There are better candidates. She got bounced from the process, you know?

FD: All will become clear. You're not Wonder Woman and we're a commercial operation. We have to hedge our bets. In fact, she's looking much more like a result than you currently do.

CH: Which means?

FD: Which means I can be a little less careful about how I get us to the end goal. Not all my eggs are in the one proverbial basket, if you know what I mean.

[Silence]

CH: Will you take us both on?

FD: Ah, the rub. Your thinking that if we take her on then you'll have no chance? Or the other way around? What do we do with her if we get our number one choice?

[Silence]

FD: We'll take you both on, if you play nice.

CH: Number one choice? What do I need to do?

FD: You need to stop planning for what happens when we get you out of those restraints. You need to start thinking about how you're going to make this all work for our equal benefit.

[Silence]

CH: What's the pension like?

FD: *[Laughter]* I'll play along. Salary is half a mil US each year, with a bonus of another half if you reach your targets within the allocated KPI limits.

CH: Interesting.

FD: Your pension, which starts when you're basically unable to carry on with the work anymore, is two hundred thousand a year. It's pretty high as not many of us make it that far. *[Laughter]*

CH: When do I start?

FD: Sorry, it's not that easy. I'm not convinced you're not going to make a break for it.

CH: What do you need me to do?

FD: Listen. Answer questions when I ask.

CH: Ask me a question. Can you take this hood off now?

212

FD: That's not me asking you. No, not yet.

[Silence, punctuated with the infrequent turning of paper]

CH: Do I still get to meet with our friend, the Doctor?

FD: Still not me asking.

[Silence, punctuated with the infrequent turning of paper]

FD: This guy, I'm afraid I'm fascinated with him. Have you figured out if he's real or just in your head?

CH: What do you think?

FD: Difficult to tell.

[Silence]

FD: I think he's real.

[Silence, punctuated with the infrequent turning of paper]

FD: Why'd you let Devlin flirt with you?

CH: Was he?

FD: Even in the dry text it's plain to see.

CH: You read the file; you'll see I'm not up with that kind of thing. Nor is he.

FD: Or are you just canny?

CH: Where's your accent from? You're doing okay at hiding it, but every so often you give off a whiff of Geordie. I knew a few of the lads in The Rifles that were from that way. Sunderland or somewhere like it, like Newcastle. They're very similar places.

FD: I'm not rising to it. And stop doing that. I ask the questions.

CH: You're not asking any.

FD: I'm sorry for the poor level of service, but we've only got one copy and we have to share it.

CH: That other guy, what's his name?

FD: Nice try.

CH: I have this thing, call it OCD. we'll have to give him a name.

[Silence]

CH: How about Kyle?

[Silence]

CH: If you're just making faces at me, I'm at a disadvantage.

FD: Why Kyle?

CH: Careless Kyle. He left his car open and lost his job.

FD: I'm sure he'd appreciate that, but I'll let you into a secret. *[Whispers]* It wasn't his only job.

CH: Oh, I'm sorry. Is he listening behind the mirror?

FD: There's no mirror.

CH: No way. There's always a one way. Anyway, I'm sorry for getting your mole fired for incompetence.

[Silence]

CH: Maybe we should call him Ian. Incompetent Ian.

[Silence]

CH: No. It doesn't have the same kind of ring to it.

FD: Your attitude is going to get you into trouble.

CH: I think it may have gone past that point, don't you?

Anyway, Kyle didn't mention you have issues with your back office.

FD: Back office?

CH: No photocopiers. I mean what sort of organisation are you asking me to join? Can't even get a photocopier in the office.

FD: We're not...

[Silence]

FB: Okay, I can see I'm going to have to be a little more careful. Look, you have a choice. Keep jabbering on and I won't have any chance to read this file.

CH: I'd rather you didn't.

FD: Why? Something you'd like me not to see?

CH: I was talking in confidence.

FD: I can see that.

[Silence]

CH: Do you want me to show you to the juicy bits?

FD: Is it full of danger and intrigue?

CH: Like a film.

FD: Which one's the bad ankle?

CH: Neither, they're both perfectly healthy.

FD: You'll have a weakness; you missed a term at Sandhurst.

CH: A precaution.

FD: Don't worry, leave it as a surprise. We can find out which is stronger a bit later on.

[Silence, punctuated with the infrequent turning of paper]

FD: Lots of my guys are old Desmonds. You'll get on with them.

CH: How did you convince them to turn to the dark side?

FD: Easy. The MOD lets them down and we pick up the pieces. Just one of the great things about the commercial sector. Private healthcare. We look after our team. We don't throw ours away when they get PTSD. We have a major programme to help stop operators burning out and it's not the dark side.

CH: *[Laughter]* Almost missed that one.

FD: Almost ignored it.

CH: How do you stop them burning out?

FD: We have a team of psychologists in on the debrief. We make sure everything you see and feel is given the time to be processed. We help you to switch off when you're not on operations.

CH: Don't they have that too?

[Silence, punctuated with the infrequent turning of paper]

FD: What you did when you were at Welbeck is famous, in certain circles of course.

CH: So I've been told.

FD: The first person to actually take a shot. I remember hearing they had to keep fleshing out the plans. They ran off script so many times. Had to pull in a load of police officers on a training exercise down the road. They'd never gone beyond the meeting at the pub before.

CH: I just went with my instincts. Look where it's landed me.

216

FD: I worry that you're a bit of a maverick. Do you like to follow the rules?

CH: It depends what the rules are.

[Silence]

FD: I bet your mind's going a million miles an hour. I bet you're thinking what you're going to do if you get out of those things around your wrist? Like you thought about how you'd deal with your imaginary friend.

CH: You're right, but I understated it to Devlin. I was planning to open him up and let him spill out in front of me.

FD: And what are you going to do to me?

CH: I haven't thought about it too much. But I reserve the right.

FD: You will.

[Silence, punctuated with the infrequent turning of paper]

CH: So how do I convince you?

FD: I know you're just trying to get this over with. Get it into your head that there is no rescue party. No one knows where you are.

CH: They'll be looking for me.

FD: And eventually they'll find you, but it will be too late to breathe life into your dead body.

CH: But what if I make it through and I join the Empire?

FD: Then the body won't be yours.

CH: I'm working with you.

FD: Okay. Tell me something that you don't want to tell me?

CH: My bra size?

FD: See.

CH: Sorry. Secrets, you mean?

FD: Yeah, why not?

CH: I've just turned twenty. I don't know any secrets about anything of use to you.

FD: What about *your* secrets?

CH: You've read Devlin's report?

FD: I've only scanned the first part.

CH: There we go, you know everything. I have no more secrets.

[Silence, punctuated with the infrequent turning of paper]

CH: I have to pee.

FD: Humph.

CH: I know your dilemma.

FD: You sat in your own piss for nearly two days already this week.

CH: And I'd do it again, but it's you that has to live with the smell. The bag gets rid of most of it for me. I'd appreciate it if I didn't have to ruin these nice jeans though. Can't keep them once you've soiled them.

FD: Soiled? How dainty. Are you a dainty girl? Are you really as innocent as you project?

CH: I've had this conversation before it would seem.

FD: What's the answer?

CH: Give me a gun and you'll see how dainty I am. Can I pee, please?

[Silence]

FD: Okay. Standard procedure, I'll be in there with you and so will three of my muckers.

CH: Can you take the bag off?

FD: Not happening, but you'll know the gun is there because it will be buried in your temple all the time.

CH: Let's hope my bladder doesn't get too shy then.

TRANSCRIPT OF AUDIO RECORDING A1763529-1
[DEVICE C120 COVERT RECORDER]

[DATE: 4th FEB 2001]
[LOCATION: 52.97865, -3.64134]

CH: Thank you, I think.

FD: You're welcome.

CH: Did you see anything you liked?

FD: Is this when the innocence ends?

CH: You tell me?

FD: Is it girls that do it for you?

CH: Sorry, I don't know I'm doing it.

FD: Instincts again.

CH: Guess so.

[Silence]

FD: Are you really an uncut diamond or just a calculating
       bitch?

CH: What's the difference? Which one gets me out of this
       situation the quickest?

FD: There's no right answer, I'm afraid.

CH: You're not being very tough with me. You're going to
       get replaced soon, I reckon.

FD: I think you might be right. I might need to give you a
       bit of pain to even things out.

CH: Let's just say you did.

FD: Oh, thanks. 'Fraid it doesn't work that way. You take
       your pick though. I can't do anything too damaging;
       broken bones take a while to heal. Means we lose

valuable operational time if you make the right decision. Flesh, on the other hand, is okay, but we have to steer clear of any major organs or it will be me on the receiving end of the treatment.

CH: They rule with an iron rod. You're not really selling it.

FD: You're right, but you should know what you're getting into. You do have a choice. A limited one, but it's still a choice.

CH: Death or service to the evil masters.

FD: I really wish you would stop saying things like that.

CH: You've made your choice then.

FD: Sorry.

[Chair scrapes against the floor]

[Dull thud and an out breath]

[Chair scrapes against the floor]

FD: I'll give you a moment.

[Silence, punctuated with the infrequent turning of paper]

CH: *[Strained words]* Where do I sign?

[Silence]

FD: Not there yet. There's quite some time to go, I'm afraid.

CH: How many are watching?

FD: I have to stay in charge of this conversation.

CH: Is the big man there? I'll talk to him if you want.

[Silence]

[Squeal of hinges and chair scraping across the floor]

CH: Oh, you're leaving? I was just beginning to like you.

[Chair scrapes against the floor and the squeal of hinges]

CH: You should get that door sorted. It's a giveaway. Unless of course it's there to unsettle me. Maybe you have a switch or a set of buttons.

[Silence]

CH: Button one must be the sound of the door's hinges, two is the sound in reverse, obviously. Ah, I hear you have a button marked 'moving a table out of the way'. I would have assumed it was bolted down.

[Silence]

CH: And one for a tall guy who doesn't get paid enough, grunting because he has to move a heavy table. He smells like the guy that got taken out because he was coming on to me. Ingenious; sounds like it's actually happening.

[Silence]

CH: Oh, that's better. It's so good to move around.

[Silence, followed by loud rustling of the bag]

CH: Nice. Hands above my head. That's new.

[Identified as David Edwards (DE), Former Trooper, Special Air Service, B Squadron (Discharged (D) 1998)]

DE: Move your feet to the side.

[Silence]

DE: Now, or I'll kick them.

[Chains rattling against the floor]

CH: Wow, that's a deep voice. You should do voice-overs.

222

[Silence]

CH: What's that around my ankles?

DE   She's talking like she's got a fucking wire. Why are you talking like you've got a wire?

[Silence]

[Unidentified Male (UM1)]

UM1:   *[Heavy French accent]* Are you going to answer the question?

CH: And a French man. De la légion sur la rivière? {*From the legion over the river?*}

DE: English.

CH: Good name for a band, don't you think?

UM1:   Was she searched?

DE: Of course, when she was out for the count.

UM1:   How thoroughly?

DE: Full pat down. Couldn't have been more thorough.

UM1:   Sure?

DE: I know her tits are real. *[Laughter]*

UM1:   Do it again. To be sure.

DE: With pleasure.

[Chains rattling against the floor]

[Chair scrapes against the floor]

[Muffled scrape of fabric]

CH: Wow, that was thorough. A girl could get the wrong idea.

[Silence]

DE: *[Loud]* Stop talking like you're a fucking nutter then. *[Chair scrapes against the floor]* She's clean.

CH: Maybe I can't. Maybe I've just gone a bit doolally. Maybe you should reconsider your offer.

UM1:   You know what that means.

CH: I was at the briefing.

UM1:   I don't think there's anything wrong with her. It's just an annoying coping mechanism.

CH: I already told the nice lady I'm ready to join. Can you take the bag off my head now?

[Slow intake of breath]

DE: No.

CH: Straight to the point.

[Outpour of air, then panting breath]

DE: Stop fucking narrating everything or it won't be in the stomach next time.

CH: I…

[Heavy laboured breathing]

CH: I...

[Laboured breath]

CH: I really don't understand what you want me to do?

UM1:   Just hang there for now. We'll do all the work.

CH: What work?

[Deep intake of breath]

CH: There's nothing to do. I'm in, I'm ready. You guys are amazing, I want to join the freedom angels or whatever you call it. Angels de liberté? {*Angels of liberty?*}

UM1:　And there you go and spoil it again.

CH:　Holy shit.

[Laboured breathy pause]

CH:　In all seriousness *[Restricted voice]*. There's something I can…

[Silence]

CH:　…tell you. That last one, the one with the cute voice… Blonde, I'm guessing, tits to die for. Am I right?

[Silence]

CH:　She asked if I had a secret, something that I could tell you to show how I'm ready to give up on the light… I mean the others, and come over to…

[Silence]

CH:　…your side.

UM1:　Is this going to be a joke?

DE:　It's okay. If it is then I'm going to take her clothes off and cavity search her.

CH:　You're wearing my clothes. I'm kidding, sorry. Humour helps with the cramps in my arms and the feeling that I'm going to shit myself if you punch me in the stomach again.

UM1:　Get on with it.

CH:　I think Stacey is already recruited.

[Silence]

UM1:   What the…?

CH: Not by them…

[Silence]

CH: …or you, I guess.

UM1:   What are you saying?

CH: I think she's a mole. She's not here to join…

[Silence]

CH: …either side.

UM1:   So what is she doing?

CH: Maybe she's from a foreign power, or even closer to home? Police maybe? Maybe she's investigating them for something?

[Deep intake of breath]

CH: Maybe she was there to interfere?

UM1:   For what purpose? In your opinion, of course.

CH: I don't know.

DE: You're not in a position to be taken seriously, I'm afraid.

CH: Have you read my file?

DE: No.

CH: Oh, yeah, the photocopier. That's a real home goal, you know. Anyway, have you got it there?

[Silence]

CH: Just tell me. You're obviously both looking at each other, thinking what to say.

[Silence]

CH: What harm is it to tell me that you have the file?

[Silence]

CH: Come on, you'll see the evidence.

[Silence]

UM1:   We have the file.

CH: Yes, I know. There's a part in the first session, I think that's where I talked about it. Stacey got back-termed in Sandhurst. She just about scraped through with her commission. She barely passed the course. Most of the exercises she succeeded in were because of my help.

[Silence]

UM1:   And? What's your point?

CH: She shouldn't have been on the course. I think she was helped through by someone up high for another reason. Another agenda.

[Silence, followed by the turning of pages]

UM1:   Okay. I see it.

CH: But what agenda I don't know.

UM1:   I'm reading.

CH: I'll let you catch up.

[Silence]

CH: I did a little digging.

[Silence]

UM1:   And what did you find?

CH: Nothing. Absolutely nothing. She wasn't clean. She was invisible.

UM1:   You're twenty years old. Why would you be able to find out anything?

CH: But you've read about the world I live in.

[Silence]

UM1:   Well that is interesting.

[Silence]

DE: You can be reasonable.

CH: Any chance I could have my seat back?

DE: No. Your ass is too nice to look at.

CH: Puis-je lui botter le cul quand je suis un membre payé. {*Can I kick his ass when I'm a paid-up member?*}

UM1:   I don't see why not.

DE: English.

CH: So am I in?

[Sound of scraping chairs and the hinges squealing]

CH: There goes that sound machine again.

[Extended silence]

[Sound of scraping chairs and the hinges squealing]

FD: I'm back.

CH: Great. Were they just covering for you so you could have a really big poo?

FD: Very good. You're going to be so much fun to work with.

CH: Can I have my seat back please?

FD: Not yet. This position seems to be working.

228

CH: Yeah, it's doing wonders for my bingo wings.

FD: *[Laughter]* I want to go over a few more things before we move on to the next phase.

CH: Shoot.

FD: Bad choice of words. I want to discuss your adoption.

CH: *[Laughter]* A cheap trick.

FD: You don't believe it.

CH: No.

FD: Have you checked?

CH: Checked how?

FD: There are ways, of course.

[Silence]

CH: Have I asked my parents? No.

FD: There are other ways... someone as resourceful as you.

CH: I didn't need to. It doesn't hold any weight. You don't think I wouldn't have known something was up?

FD: Sure, but we have information.

[Silence]

FD: I don't know how to break this to you.

[Silence]

FD: What's wrong? Why are you tensing up?

CH: Just stomach cramps. I'm fine, unless you want to punch me in the stomach again that is.

[Silence]

FD: It's fine for now. Look, we have information.

CH: Right. You're loving this.

FD: It doesn't give me a sense of joy, honest.

CH: Scout's honour?

FD: It's real, I'm afraid.

CH: That's lazy. Cheap. They couldn't convince me so I'm not sure why you think you can. Anyway, why does it really matter?

FD: I haven't been twiddling my thumbs while you've been winding my colleagues up. Do you still remember what happened when that guy tried to kidnap you?

CH: Like I'm going to forget.

FD: So you do?

CH: As if it happened yesterday.

FD: Remind me.

CH: You have the details in front of you.

FD: Humour me. I can start testing out your ankles if you prefer.

CH: First time or second?

FD: Both. One at a time.

CH: I would be able to think better if my hands weren't tied above my head.

FD: I think your focus is fine.

[Silence]

CH: He was waiting in the toilets. Grabbed me with an arm around my waist and a hand over my mouth.

FD: Did he hurt you?

CH: Of course he did. He was grabbing tight.

FD: How did it hurt? Take your time.

CH: He was grabbing me.

FD: He was holding you, stopping you running off.

CH: Yes.

FD: But did he actually hurt you? Punch you, scratch you? Was there a knife? Did he cut you?

[Silence]

CH: My instinct is to say yes, but…

[Silence]

CH: I don't remember any real pain. What's your point?

FD: There's something wrong here. My colleagues agree. Something not quite right.

CH: What do you mean?

FD: There are so many other ways he could have done this. So many ways that would have guaranteed success.

CH: Like?

FD: Let me turn that around on you. If you were going to kidnap a young girl, how would you go about it?

CH: I wouldn't.

FD: Don't be so sure. It's not beyond either of our organisations to require as much.

[Silence]

FD: Take your time.

[Silence]

CH: I'd do it somewhere quieter.

FD: Agreed, but if it had to be at that school and at that time?

CH: I'd drug them. Chloroform or something similar.

FD: Yeah, or what I used on you. *[Laughter]* But seriously, it's a bit trickier to get the right dosage for kids.

CH: Sure.

FD: I can understand why that was left out. What else?

CH: Knock them out.

FD: Yep, that's what we thought, too. Much less of a chance of getting caught or you getting away.

CH: What's your point?

FD: My point is, if you didn't want to risk the drugs then you would knock them out, or gag them or something. What you don't do is let them kick and fight back.

CH: So he wasn't very good.

FD: How about the second time?

CH: He had more help. A sack or a blanket was thrown over me, covering my head all the way down to my arms.

FD: And yet you escaped.

CH: Because I'd had training in self-defence.

FD: Two grown men couldn't overpower a thirteen-year-old girl?

CH: I was strong, determined. I had more to lose than

232

they had to gain. Your point?

FD: He didn't want to hurt you. In fact, he was doing everything in his power not to harm even a tiny little hair on your head.

[Silence]

FD: Have you thought about that before?

CH: Are you related to Dr Devlin?

FD: Answer the question.

[Silence]

CH: Because he wanted me perfect?

FD: Why?

CH: His fetish? I don't know. I don't get what this has got to do with your adoption obsession?

FD: Did they show you his file?

CH: Whose file?

FD: Your natural father's.

CH: No, they said it was too big to fit in the room.

FD: Not much of an exaggeration to be fair. He's been trying to get to you for years, racking up all sorts of problems along the way.

CH: And I knew nothing about this. *[Laughter]*

FD: Not so perceptive after all.

CH: *[Exaggerated laughter]* The penny just dropped. *[Laughter]* I get it.

FD: It took you long enough.

CH: You're saying this guy, the guy that actually nearly killed me twice, is my long-lost daddy. That's where your fantasy falls apart. Why the hell would my so-called real father want to kidnap me?

FD: Because he's your father and he's not allowed to see you.

CH: Why isn't he allowed to see me?

FD: Order of the court. He's not allowed to contact you. It's the law.

[Silence]

FD: I'll give you a minute.

CH: Don't need a minute. I still don't get it. I nearly died, nearly got run over. I was so close. That fucker destroyed my fucking dreams.

FD: This is the first time we've really seen you getting emotional?

CH: I'm not emotional.

[Silence]

CH: Just an expressive moment.

[Silence]

CH: I'm back now.

FD: Most people would have crumbled in a heap.

CH: Had they not had their hands tied over their heads.

FD: You, of course, know exactly what I mean. You are an exceptional person.

CH: So I keep being told. Look where it gets me.

FD: Next time, you know to be more observant.

CH: You mean notice the guy behind me shoving the

syringe into my neck?

FD: You put yourself at risk.

CH: I didn't know I was at risk.

FD: You know now, but that doesn't matter. You've not been trained. The training we'll give you is second to none.

CH: What, better than I would have had?

FD: We practically have the same programme, the same people who'd run it before, in the most part, but with a little twist here and more diversity there. Look, my point was we know he's your dad and if I were you, I would start coming to terms with it as a distinct possibility.

CH: It's kind of difficult to look at anything at the moment.

FD: Your stomach again?

CH: And the cramps in my arms and sweat running into my eyes.

[Silence]

FD: Suck it up.

CH: I hope the welfare's better when I'm official.

[Sound of scraping chairs and the hinges squealing]

[Long silence]

[Sound of hinges squealing]

CH: They require more convincing, don't they.

[Silence]

CH: I don't need to see your face.

FD: Yes.

CH: How's Stacey doing?

FD: She's doing well. It's all wrapped up. I saw her just
        now.

[Silence]

CH: Can I see her?

FD: Not at the moment, although I might bring her in so
        she can tell you all about the virtues of joining in her
        own words.

CH: Why not now?

FD: There's something I've got to do.

[Silence]

FD: It's part of the process. I was hoping you would be
        able to convince them it wasn't necessary.

CH: I'm intrigued.

[Silence]

CH: What are you doing?

FD: Now, if you try and kick me I'm going to cause you a
        lot of pain and I'll have to ruin your nice clothes.

[Silence]

CH: Do you realise how much self-control this takes not
        to knee you in the face?

FD: I thought we were friends?

CH: Hey, maybe in another setting this could be fun, but
        my arms are kind of tired.

[Muffled squeal of pain and scuffling]

FD: Fucking bitch.

CH: You're not taking my fucking clothes off without a fi….

[Breath pulled from lungs, heavy breathing]

CH: They were my favourite.

[Unidentified Male (UM2)]

UM2:   Shut the fuck up, bitch. *[Sounds of scuffling]* Oh, for fuck sake.

CH: Sorry, I needed another pee.

UM2:   It's all over my hands. For fuck's sake.

[Unidentified Male (UM3)]

UM3:   What do you want to do?

UM1:   Shut the fuck up.

CH: Hey, no need to on my part. That tickles.

UM3:   This'll tickle.

[Breath pulled from lungs]

UM2:   Ooh, that looks like a nasty scar on you belly.

CH: Fucking touch that and I'll…

FD: Grab hold of her *[Muffled sounds of a struggle]* legs. Fasten that to the ground eye.

UM2:   It's covered in piss.

FD: *[Shouts]* Get the fucking hose.

[Water spray, audio muffled]

CH: *[muffled]* Okay, okay, I'm sorry.

FD: *[muffled]* Don't be fucking sorry, you stupid bitch.

Bring in Stacey.

[Muffled squeal of hinges back and forth]

[Identified as Stacey Silvers (SS) (Alias), Candidate Section A (Discharged (H) ██████████████████████████████ ███████████████████████████, *See File Annex X34223109-81, X9727261-8, X-67129091-12, X-8819301-1)]*

SS: *[muffled]* Oh my god, what have they done to you?

FD: *[muffled]* Stand back. Don't move over that line. Remember what we said.

SS: *[muffled]* Okay, okay. Shit, girl, what the hell are they doing to you?

CH: *[muffled]* Are you okay?

SS: *[muffled]* I'm fine.

CH: *[muffled]* Is it true what they're saying?

SS: *[muffled]* What are they saying? Can we get her a towel or something?

CH: *[muffled]* Are you sure you're okay?

SS: Not even a bruise.

[Pause and muffled loud coughing]

CH: And you're comfortable with betraying everything you've been working for these last few years?

SS: It's not like that. Fucking hell, look at the state of you.

CH: Can you get them to take off the hood?

SS: They won't listen to me.

FD: She's right, we won't.

SS: Look, it's just like they said. It's the same job, but just in the private sector. I wasn't going to get into that place anyway.

CH: You could have reapplied.

SS: It doesn't work like that.

CH: How can you be so sure?

SS: That's what they told me when I asked.

CH: When did you ask? I thought you didn't make it back from London?

SS: They made contact, eventually.

CH: You could have shown them you were right for the job.

SS: I failed.

CH: You shouldn't have taken no for an answer.

SS: Kicking off would have got me nowhere.

CH: You're right, but maybe there was something you could have done to show them that what happened was just a blip. Fuck me, you just lost your rag once.

[Silence]

SS: I didn't think of that. Anyway, I don't think I was their kind of person.

CH: Yeah. Okay, it's fine just to give it all up.

SS: It's too late, I guess.

CH: Well it is now.

[Silence]

CH: You didn't take much convincing.

SS: We all have our buttons. They pressed the right ones

and I saw pretty quickly that this was a good option to me.

CH: A good option? I guess the process worked.

SS: What do you mean by that?

CH: I mean, I'm the one strung up like a prize turkey, completely naked apart from a bag over my head and to be really honest, I haven't swallowed one iota of this bollocks. How long did it take for you to throw away everything you believe in?

SS: I told you, I have my buttons. Look, Corra, I don't think you should say any more. These guys look pretty pissed.

CH: I don't know why they're the ones with the hump. Don't they like what they see? Are they not getting enough blood to their balls?

SS: Do me a favour and stop with the bullshit. We know you're going to come along with the ride. We know it's going to happen. Just make it easy on yourself and do what you're going to do anyway.

CH: Wow, chill the shit out. Am I keeping you from something? What makes you think I'll make that choice?

SS: Join or die? You have a chance not to be dead.

CH: How do you know which I'll choose?

SS: You'll make the choice any sane person would.

CH: But they'll always know that I couldn't be trusted.

SS: You shouldn't say that.

CH: It's true and they know it.

SS: They'll make you show them, after a little more

convincing.

CH: They don't know my buttons.

SS: Don't be so sure.

CH: What were your buttons, Stacey?

SS: They're personal.

CH: Personal? Between you and me? We're kind of past that, aren't we?

SS: Sorry, but you may not know me quite as well as you think you do.

FD: This is very touching, but we're getting off the point. We're going to have to take this up a level; time is our enemy. Stacey, you take a seat.

SS: Does she have to be naked?

CH: Don't bother, Stacey. You're on the bottom rung. You're at least a couple of days before overtaking her, then it'll be your turn to do this.

FD: Time to shut the fuck up. Grab that hose.

SS: I would stop painting these people as the bad guys.

CH: *[Laughter]*

SS: The others aren't so squeaky clean. How do you think they get information out of people that don't want to give it? Are you really that naive?

CH: I don't think this is part of their programme. Do you truthfully think it is? They get enough volunteers and don't need to snatch people off the streets. Anyway, I'm getting bored now. Bring in your boss and we'll have a chat. I'll give him my decision and then you can do whatever you need to do.

FD: And why do you think we would do that?

241

CH: I know he's watching this. You know he's watching
        this. Get him in, then I can talk directly, rather
        through a monkey.

FD: I'm in charge.

CH: Pleeeease.

FD: What? Don't you think a woman could do this?

CH: Do you have eyes? Of course I think a woman could
        be in charge of the Death Star. I just don't think *you*
        could be in charge.

[Silence]

FD: Did you talk to Stacey about him?

SS: Who?

FD: The mystery man.

SS: Corra?

CH: No, I didn't. There was no need. That's my past.

FD: Not according to what you said to Devlin. Read this.

CH: No.

[Silence]

CH: Please.

SS: They're not giving me a choice.

[Silence, punctuated with the infrequent turning of paper]

SS: What's wrong?

CH: Other than the obvious?

SS: Come on.

CH: Just stomach cramps.

FD: You fucking shit on my floor then that hose is going up your ass.

[Silence, punctuated with the infrequent turning of paper]

SS: I could have helped you.

CH: I didn't need your help.

SS: You seemed to open up to Devlin.

CH: He's a professional busy body. I had no choice.

FD: Once the scab was off, you wouldn't shut up about it.

CH: You can have your opinion.

FD: Here, read this part.

SS: I don't think I need to see that.

FD: No, I think you'll get an insight into your friend.

CH: Does she need insight?

FD: Maybe she has an opinion on your invisible friend.

SS: Huh.

[Silence, punctuated with the infrequent turning of paper]

FD: Well, does he or doesn't he exist? What do you think?

CH: I thought you've already made your mind up. He's my long-lost sperm father, according to you.

FD: I wonder if Stacey has a different opinion.

CH: What does it matter? Do we really have to do this while I'm like this? How about we thrash this out over a couple of margaritas? Maybe a bite to eat? I'll be much more amenable.

FD: Well, if you're still alive in a week or two then I'd love to, but I'm afraid we've got a long way to go.

SS: How could he not be real?

[Silence]

CH: You didn't see him.

SS: When?

CH: The café during the London operation.

SS: Right after you stole my flag?

[Silence]

SS: I remember you asking…

[Silence]

SS: …but I only took a glance. I was really distracted. To be honest I was shit scared about the progress we were making. I knew against you I was screwed. I barely looked.

[Silence]

CH: Shit. Fuck.

[Silence]

CH: That's what finally convinced me it was all in my head. Fuck sake.

SS: I'm sorry.

[Silence]

SS: Is that where you had your appendix out? Just before we met.

CH: *[Barely audible]* Yeah.

SS: I'm sorry. I should have been paying more attention.

[Silence]

SS: I guess that's why you were going to make it and I was

244

out.

[Silence]

CH: I don't care who he is. I'm going to kill that son of a
       bitch.

FD: I'm going to let you take a rest.

CH: What?

*[Pause, muffled movement and keys turning in locks, followed by muffled
movement]*

CH: Thank you. What about the bag?

FD: In a minute. Take a moment, sit down here.

CH: What's changed?

FD: You've accepted it. You've accepted he's real.

CH: Now you're going to tell me he's not, right?

FD: He's real all right.

CH: You seem so sure.

FD: He's next door.

[Silence]

CH: What the fuck? All along? Why? Why not just bring
       the cunt in from the beginning? *[Deep pulls of air]* Why
       is he here?

FD: He's yours. A gift.

CH: What?

FD: He's next door for you.

CH: You want me to talk to him?

FD: If you want. You can thrash it out if that's how you
       want to sign this off.

CH: So he does work for you?

FD: No.

CH: Then how?

FD: We hunted him down.

CH: Why? What for?

FD: To give him to you.

CH: No, I don't get it.

FD: He's yours to do what you want with.

CH: You know what I want to do.

FD: And that's fine, too.

CH: You'd do that?

FD: We look after our own.

CH: You want me to kill him?

FD: You want to kill him, you said that.

[Silence]

FD: Or were those just words?

[Silence]

FD: If you kill him then we'll know.

CH: Know what?

FD: That you're going to come to us. That you're going to
        make it through this.

CH: How?

FD: I'll give you a gun.

CH: You'll give me a gun? You trust me?

FD: We'll be fine. One bullet, that's all you need.

CH: And then?

FD: Then we'll do what you want.

CH: We'll take a break?

FD: We'll take a break, or talk, if you want.

CH: Okay.

[Squeal of door hinges, opening]

[Silence]

[A heavy but soft thump slaps on to the floor]

[Squeal of door hinges and heavy breath]

CH: Shit.

FD: It's okay. Take the bag off, let her see his face.

[Gasp]

[Muffled sound of a deep voice]

FD: Shut the fuck up.

CH: Oh my god, this is real. It's bright in here.

[Silence]

CH: Ah, the door's real, too. You have better décor than the other guys. Still no plants though.

SS: Very real. Are you okay?

CH: I'll be fine.

FD: It's real. Now you can shoot him in the head.

CH: I was wrong about your hair, but not everything else.

[Silence]

[Heavy object clanking on the thin metal of the table]

CH: I want him to suffer.

FD: Stomach then. Slow and painful.

CH: Chain him to the ceiling. Leave the gag on. Has he been searched?

FD: For what? He'd have been frisked.

CH: Nothing.

FD: Do as she says.

CH: Everyone out.

FD: As she says.

CH: You, too.

[Silence]

CH: You can stay if you want, but I'll have a loaded gun.

FD: I don't think I need to worry, but as you wish. We'll be watching and listening.

SS: Do you want me to stay?

CH: No. This is personal. But…

[Silence]

FD: Yes?

CH: After this I want to meet him or her, or whoever it is. I want to look them in the eye. Then I'll know.

[Silence]

[Squeal of door hinges]

[Scraping against the table]

[Snap and click of dull plastic]

[Muffled breath in the background getting louder]

[Loud, deep slow breaths]

CH: Well, here we are. One bullet. One man.

[Silence]

[Ruffle of clothing]

CH: *[Barely audible]* Now.

[Thud of something light hitting the floor]

[Snap click]

CH: *[Loud]* I wish I could ask you why.

[Silence]

[Click]

CH: *[Loud]* I wish I could know the truth, but I don't think you'd tell me.

[Silence]

[Click]

CH: I want you to know you're going to die.

[Silence]

[Click]

CH: It's going to be slow and painful.

[Muffled breath increasing in ferocity, inaudible speech]

[Click]

CH: I don't care what you say.

[Muffled breaths getting faster and faster]

[Silence]

[Loud gunshot]

[Silence]

CH: Is that painful enough? I don't think so.

[Muffled scream of pain followed by heavy muffled panting]

CH: Fuck, I've got blood all over my hand now.

[Squeal of the door hinges]

[Silence]

FD: You must feel better now?

CH: You sound like that cunt, Devlin.

FD: You'll get your chance with him. I'll hold him to one side for you.

CH: He's not…?

FD: No. Bloody hell. Is he dead?

CH: Not yet. Where's the boss?

FD: She's standing in front of you.

[Silence]

CH: Stacey.

SS: How'd…?

CH: *[Laughter]*

SS: Why are you laughing?

FD: Pressure release.

CH: *[Laughter]* No. You're the heir to the empire. Aren't you?

SS: How long have you known?

CH: Suspected for a while. You just confirmed it.

SS: For how long?

CH: Since Sandhurst.

[Silence]

SS: I don't understand. Why didn't you just agree then?

CH: Why didn't *you* just ask me?

SS: You had to join because you wanted to and not just
        because we're friends.

CH: Are we friends?

[Silence]

SS: What? I thought that was obvious.

CH: Was it real, or was it part of the plan?

SS: For me it was…

[Silence]

SS: …real. You?

[Silence]

CH: No.

[Silence]

SS: What do you mean?

CH: I sought you out.

SS: I found *you*. The lonely child on the course for mean
        adults. You were cowering in the corner and I came
        to your rescue.

CH: I let you come to me.

SS: What do you mean? What does she mean? You were
        back-termed, like me. We met because we both were
        injured.

CH: For the head of an international criminal gang you're
        not very bright.

SS: But *you* were back-termed?

CH: I had to go off somewhere and it helped with the
        timing no end.

SS: To have your appendix removed.

CH: Yes.

SS: You nearly died. That's what you said. That's what
        they said.

CH: That is what I said.

SS: But that's not real?

CH: No. I just had to make space.

[Silence]

SS: Where is this going? How did you find out who I am?

CH: You have no clue. She has no clue.

[Silence]

SS: *[Shouts]* How did you know? Goddamit.

CH: I was told.

SS: *[Shouts]* By who?

CH: By my employers, of course.

FD: To make room for what?

SS: Yeah, for what?

CH: A recorder.

SS: Recording what?

CH: The sound from the microphone in the corner of my

252

eye.

FD: The black eyes.

CH: Yes. An annoying side effect.

SS: What the hell? What are you telling me?

CH: I'm telling you I knew I'd be here.

SS: Here? What? What for?

CH: To find you.

SS: We brought you here.

CH: Precisely.

SS: *[Shouts]* What for?

CH: To stop you doing what you're doing. To stop you recruiting our best and turning them against us.

SS: You? Us? What do you mean? What does she mean?

CH: Your mistake was being greedy. You took too many of us, or tried. Too many recruits were going missing.

FD: She means she's already recruited, for them. She's operational.

SS: What?

FD: We've been set up.

[Barely audible low rumbling background noise]

SS: What's that noise?

CH: That's the second thing I had installed.

FD: A tracker.

CH: Gold star. And the recorder for the microphone. I had to give them time.

SS: I thought she was searched?

FD: She was. I can't see it and she's naked. So who have you just killed?

CH: A colleague.

SS: But you killed him.

CH: It looks bad, doesn't it, but he'll be fine.

SS: You fucking stupid cunt.

CH: The penny drops.

SS: We'll take out each one of those mother fucking pricks and split them wide. You think you can play me like a fool? You made me waste a whole fucking year on your pathetic little ass and your self-righteous piety for their stupid fucking cause. We could have been good together. We could have made a storm. We could have made a fuck tonne of money and had a fucking good laugh ripping this world open. You stupid cunt.

CH: I didn't think you liked me this much. For that I'm sorry.

SS: Keep your fucking sorrow. That's no good to me. It's going to be a shame to kill you, but I'll remember the good times and what could have been.

[Silence]

SS: You won't get away with this. The whole place is locked from the inside.

CH: I know.

FD: Um, Stacey. I don't think …

SS: Shut the fuck up.

FD: I don't think that gun is empty.

254

SS: Don't be so fucking stupid. It had one round. You loaded it yourself.

[Loud bang]

SS: What the fuck? How did you...? You were searched.

CH: I was, but you didn't do a thorough job on Daddy.

[Silence]

SS: He had bullets on him.

CH: Yeah. It's a good job you gave me the same calibre, otherwise this was going to be a whole lot harder.

SS: I thought I knew you.

[Silence]

SS: What do you think you're going to achieve? I'm not going to jail.

CH: You're right.

FD: She's here to kill us.

CH: You're right again. *[Loud bang]* And dead.

SS: What the fuck? You can't be serious. You can't do this. We're friends. We spoke every night; we lay on each other's beds talking into the night. Don't you remember all of the things we were going to do together when all of that was over?

CH: I really got to you, didn't I?

SS: Don't you remember that night we almost...?

CH: I remember. I liked you. I like you, but you're a bitch. Or will be.

SS: I don't get it. Why all this charade? We can be bitches together. Can't we?

[Silence]

SS: Please, Corra, come here. We're not bad people.

CH: You are from where I'm standing.

[Loud bang]

[Loud bang]

TRANSCRIPT OF AUDIO RECORDING A1763529-1
[DEVICE C120 COVERT RECORDER]

[DATE:6th FEB 2001] [13:00GMT]
[LOCATION: ███████████████████████ *]*

DD: You look better than I thought you would.

CH: Thanks, I think. It'll heal. So this is your office? Much nicer than that windowless box we were in. These chairs are much more comfortable.

DD: Yes. Despite my protests, CAPOP didn't want any of you getting comfortable. He thinks the candidates would just sleep throughout our conversations.

[Silence]

DD: I've read your report. Operation Dawn Wolf. You were the wolf?

CH: I guess, and the Dawn. ████████ chose it. He had to explain that dawn was for me being a recruit and wolf for the sheep's clothing thing.

DD: Had you never heard that saying? From the New Testament, I think.

[Silence]

DD: Are those things still in there?

CH: I'm getting them removed tomorrow.

DD: Are you okay?

CH: I'm fine. Looking forward to a week in bed.

DD: I won't take long. No more reports. This is just checking you're okay, like any other debriefing.

CH: It's fine.

DD: How did you know they were going to give you a gun?

CH: I didn't, but the whole operation was aimed about getting me in that room with a weapon. Unlikely they would give me a knife; it's reusable. A gun, on the other hand, can only be used so many times.

DD: Unless you had bullets hidden away.

CH: As long as they were the right size. I couldn't have been more relieved when they put the Glock on the table.

DD: You must have had a back-up plan?

CH: I would have had to show them my jujitsu skills, until I could find another weapon.

[Silence]

DD: How did you know I wasn't involved?

CH: I didn't. Actually, at one time I thought you might have been in charge, but you've been cleared now, I'm told.

DD: You thought I might have been in charge whilst we were talking?

CH: The thought crossed my mind. Especially when you gave me the book.

DD: *[Laughter]* Surely you must have suspected I was something to do with it when you realised they had the transcripts of our sessions?

CH: No. They were meant to get to them. How else would they know my inner workings? We had guys on the inside, too.

[Silence]

DD: I feel like I've been played. *[Laughter]*

CH: I'm sorry if you feel that way, but it was necessary.

258

DD: I understand. I'm just processing, that's all.

CH: Do you want to swap seats?

DD: *[Laughter]* I thought I got to know you pretty well, but was that really you? Was it all made up?

CH: It was the real me, just with a few details switched up.

[Silence]

DD: Who was the guy?

CH: A rock hard SBS. A volunteer, no less.

DD: I hear he's doing okay.

CH: He's fine. Once they took the Kevlar plate from his stomach they confirmed only bruising. A couple of weeks rest, then light duties for a while and he'll be fine. He said the worst bit was when I had to swirl my finger in the hole so I could cover up the white of the plating. Hurt like hell.

DD: Gymnastics?

CH: True.

DD: The ankle?

CH: Yeah, true.

DD: The attempted kidnap?

CH: Afraid not. I fell off a swing and sheared my ankle. Not quite so dramatic, but still the same end. The whole thing about the stalker was made up, I'm afraid.

DD: The Cadet Corp?

CH: All true. Welbeck, as well. The Chadwick Challenge was all real. They came back to me after my first term at Sandhurst and took me off. No appendicitis though, just intense training for two months, then the op. It was pretty uncomfortable.

DD: But the scar was real?

CH: Yes. The recorder is partially sown in but I can open the scar to add new tapes and batteries. You want to see before they put me back together?

DD: Ah, no thanks. You wore that thing for over a year?

CH: Yeah. Can't wait to get it gone. You may have noticed me needing to take a break. I was always worried about the tapes or the batteries running out.

[Silence]

DD: Do you remember when I asked you if you would kill someone?

CH: Yes.

DD: Were you telling the truth then?

CH: Yes.

DD: How does it sit with you?

CH: They were bad people. I was fully briefed.

[Silence]

CH: My job was to find them and cut the head off the beast. I was fine with that, much as I said I would be.

[Silence]

DD: Isn't that the Judge Dredd scenario?

CH: No. The punishment has already been decided. I was just there to find out who needed to be punished.

[Silence]

DD: ███████ ████. I remembered him.

260

[Silence]

CH: Yes. He was real.

DD: I did his analysis, as I did for you.

CH: I know.

DD: I realise now it was you he talked about.

CH: Don't.

[Silence]

CH: Please.

[Silence]

DD: And that's how we recruited you.

CH: Yes. Imagine you're eighteen and being shown pictures of your childhood hero cut into quarters, his body tortured almost beyond recognition.

DD: I don't think anyone should have to see that.

CH: I'm glad I saw it; I asked them to show me. I'm glad they told me what they'd done. I'm glad that even after all they did to him, he didn't give up on what he believed in.

DD: Is that what drove you to this?

CH: Drove is not the right word, but yes. It's what motivated me and it's what will keep me going.

[Silence]

CH: My only stipulation was that my family would be guaranteed to stay safe in all this.

DD: Of course, but how could they?

CH: They built me a new life; well, two new lives. They gave me a cover, then built on top of that. If you find

out who I really am, you'd still be wrong. The
adoption was part of that and we knew they would
think it gave them leverage. A way in.

        Still, when they used it in Tactical
Questioning it took me by surprise, made me feel…
made me feel my family were so vulnerable. I haven't
been called ▮▮▮ in so long. My reaction, in the most
part, was genuine.

DD: And you played it very well. It makes your
accomplishment of coming through Tactical
Questioning much greater. You never revealed your
new identity.

[Silence]

DD: I have to ask, who knew here? Did they let you get
away with all those things?

CH: No one knew in the training team; we didn't know
who was involved. Only a handful above knew what
I was actually doing.

DD: Wow.

CH: Thanks.

DD: Was it worth it?

CH: I'd do it again tomorrow.

DD: You need to talk this over.

CH: I will, but just not yet.

DD: Don't leave it forever, or you'll be saving up the
problems to kick you in the ass in years to come.

[Silence]

DD: At least now I understand why I always got the
sense you were holding something back.

[Silence]

DD: What else is true?

CH: I guess you'll find out soon enough.

DD: I'll be seeing you around then?

CH: Yep. I'm on the team. Just like the other guy that passed.

DD: No. Not just like him at all.

[Silence]

DD: One last question? What do I call you?

CH: Carrie Harris.

DD: Agent Carrie Harris. That has a nice ring to it.

CH: Doesn't it just. Thank you, Dr Devlin.

DD: Call me David. Please.

END OF TRANSCRIPT OF AUDIO RECORDING A1763529-1.

TRANSCRIPT OF AUDIO RECORDING A1632313-1.

DOWNLOADED 3ʳᵈ MARCH 1999, TRANSCRIBED 4ᵗʰ MARCH 1999, SECTION D ▇▇▇▇▇▇▇▇▇▇▇

[DATE: 2ⁿᵈ March 1999]
[LOCATION: M4 Westbound Near Junction 4]

[Identified as ▇▇▇▇▇▇ ▇▇▇▇▇▇▇▇ *(A1), Head of Service,*
▇▇▇▇▇▇▇▇▇▇▇

A1:   You are a very special woman.

[Identified as ▇▇ ▇▇▇▇▇▇▇ *(AW)]*

AW: Thank you.

A1:   I'm not here just to give you compliments, but I have a few more. You have a certain set of skills which I don't think you even know about, but believe me we do. Those skills could potentially make you into a very valuable ally. What are your plans for the future?

AW: Ah, thank you, I think. I've joined the Army. I've been accepted at Sandhurst.

A1:   What regiment are you going for?

AW: I don't know yet, but I'm thinking maybe the Royal Engineers, or something like that.

A1:   Ever thought of the Intelligence Corp?

AW: Thought about it, but it's very difficult to get into.

A1:   And you don't think you could?

AW: I don't know. I haven't looked into the detail.

A1:   I think you would be the first pick.

AW: I don't know about that.

A1:   Army recruits usually fall into three camps; those that

264

have no ambition and just pick their home regiment, then there are those that want to be super humans in the paras and those that want to be the super brains in the Intelligence Corp. You'd do well in either.

AW: I haven't thought that far ahead. I've still got a year before I have to choose.

A1:   You do, but there is an alternative.

AW: To the Intelligence Corp?

A1:   To the Army.

AW: I'm already enrolled.

A1:   Good, that would be part of the deal.

AW: What deal?

A1:   If you were to join our organisation.

AW: I'm not being rude, but I have no idea what you're talking about?

A1:   I'm sorry, but the nature of our world means I have to decide at what stage you are ready to be told where I work and at where I am offering you a position.

AW: Is it the Security Service?

A1:   It is a security service.

AW: SIS?

A1:   No, neither of those and not GCHQ. We are another organisation that works for the protection of the Crown of the UK and our allies.

AW: Interpol?

A1:   No. We are not the police. I wouldn't bother guessing.

AW: You're a truly secret service?

A1:   You could say that.

AW: So what's the job?

A1:   We'll get to that.

AW: What are these skills that make me so suited to this super-secret role?

A1:   For one, you are extremely observant. You notice things that other people don't. You seem to have a suspicious mind and you're not afraid to get involved. You're a little reckless, but training will help with that.

AW: If you're trying to make me blush then you might be succeeding.

A1:   You've shown that your potential for military skills is beyond question. Tactics, fieldcraft, leadership, I know of a number of regiments and organisations in the queue behind me, some of which you have already mentioned.

AW: You realise they would tell me exactly what they were offering.

A1:   No, they wouldn't. They'd be asking you where you want to work. What do you see yourself doing with your life, in the Army or otherwise?

AW: Work for a few years and then have a family. Retire early somewhere hot.

A1:   I... I hope you're joking.

AW: I am. You can add a keen sense of humour to that list. I'm only just seventeen, but still I can't see myself with a string of kids around my neck.

A1:   You might change your mind.

AW: That, of course, would be my right. Are you worried that I'll take your job and fall in love a few days later and give it all up?

A1:   No. You have too much drive for that.

AW: I can't think of anything worse. Men haven't been a feature in my life so far.

A1:   How close are you to your family?

AW: Average, I suppose, but I don't have a great deal to go on. You might say I'm a loner, which I guess would be a benefit?

A1:   Yes and no. You don't make friends easily?

AW: Too easily, but there isn't time to get into that now. Let's just say if I wanted to I could, but I choose to focus on my career. My choice.

A1:   How would you feel about lying to your family?

AW: About what? I can keep a secret, if that's what you mean?

A1:   I mean not telling them anything about what you'll do. I mean not speaking to them for months at a time, for their own safety. How do you feel about changing your name, having a new identity, a new history? How do you feel about wiping the slate clean and starting from scratch?

AW: I haven't said no.

A1:   Do you want to be in the movies?

AW: I couldn't think of anything worse.

A1:   Do you want glamour and fame?

AW: No. I wouldn't say I'm a typical teenager.

A1:   What do you want then?

AW: I want to be good at what I do. I want to make a

difference.

A1:   And what if you make a difference but no one gets to know?

AW: I'll know.

A1:   What are your hobbies?

AW: Hobbies? If you mean what do I do when I'm not at college or studying, I'll be on the range learning a new weapon or tightening up my shots, or I'd be running or in the gym. Maybe reading a good book.

A1:   What do you like to read?

AW: Mills and Boon.

A1:   You're joking again.

AW: Of course. Anything really, the classics. Have you heard of a new novelist called Lee Child? I'm nearly through Stephen King's back catalogue.

A1:   You could still do those things.

AW: So are we talking trial period and see how things go?

A1:   It doesn't work like that, I'm afraid. We have a well prescribed process you would usually have to go through first, but we have something else in mind for you; something that will help us out no end.

AW: But?

A1:   But it means a lot of sacrifices and you'd have to get up to speed really quickly. Then you'd have to go through hell, probably quite a few times.

AW: I think I've already made my decision. When do I start?

A1:   We'll be in touch.

END OF TRANSCRIPT OF AUDIO RECORDING A1632313-1.

END OF CASE FILE ID65461097-01-ODW

GJ
STEVENS

LESSON
LEARNED

AN
AGENT CARRIE HARRIS
ACTION THRILLER

www.gjstevens.com

Want more of Agent Carrie Harris? Check out **Lesson Learned.**

New recruit Agent Carrie Harris is deployed on assignment at last, but instead of the cut and thrust of a sprawling city, hunting the worst enemies of the state, she is placed as an au pair living with a family in the middle of nowhere, left only with two simple commands ringing in her ears.

Observe. Report.

After surviving the highly secret Special Operations candidate selection process, along with her first assignment (OPERATION DAWN WOLF), Carrie finds the slow pace of life difficult to adjust to. At first unsettled by the calm, she slowly relaxes into the distractions of suburban living and friendships blossom in the unlikeliest of places.

As the weeks go by still not knowing her purpose and with nothing other than the mundane to report, will Carrie keep focused when the tedious veneer cracks to reveal the deplorable reason for her dispatch? Can she be ready to act, ditching the temptation to make her cover story real, or revert to be the honed, ruthless operator again? Will she make the right choices or be sucked into a different life, distracted by a passion which threatens to overwhelm her?

Visit **gjstevens.com** for news about new releases and sign up to the mailing list to receive free books!

gjstevens.com
